HIDDEN PAST

Hidden Past

A Romantic Suspense Novel

Sidney Lanier

Library of Congress Control Number:		2018902831
ISBN:	Hardcover	978-1-9845-1324-3
	Softcover	978-1-9845-1326-7
	eBook	978-1-9845-1325-0

Print information available on the last page.

Rev. date: 04/04/2018

To order additional copies of this book, contact:
Xlibris
1-888-795-4274
www.Xlibris.com
Orders@Xlibris.com
774266

HIDDEN PAST is dedicated to my mother Betty, who always believed in me, no matter what.

HIDDEN PAST
MAIN CHARACTERS

Angela Capelli Morris – A beautiful woman who grew up in Gallipolis, Ohio

Austin Morris – Angela's gentlemanly husband who grew up in Medina, Ohio

Kenny Chessin – Angela's first boyfriend

Red Conway – A wealthy man whom Angela dates

Fredrik Werner – A young man whom Angela goes out with once

Lorena Weiss – Austin's employer (and more) at the campus of Ohio State University

Len Weiss – Lorena's husband who passed away before she ever met Austin

Allan Federer – The attorney and chairman of the corporation owned by Lorena Weiss

Sashi Rinaldi – A waitress at the Victory Circle

Janie Rosen – A social worker who grew up in Shaker Heights, Ohio

Elinor and Harry Rosen – Janie's parents

Sheldon Ksonska – A childhood friend and secret admirer of Janie, now a trust officer managing the Rosens' trust fund

PART I

CHAPTER 1

Angela Morris was beautiful and seemed especially soft and alluring in the evening of the Naples Philharmonic fund-raiser. She was calm, more relaxed than usual, and had no clue that a voice from her past would torpedo her comfort tonight and threaten her now perfect existence in the future.

"You are absolutely stunning!" Angela's tall, tanned, impeccably dressed husband Austin told her as the chauffer eased the limo away from the circular drive. Austin Morris could not have been any more proud of his wife. He was totally comfortable with his wife of three years, but he knew she was not always comfortable with herself.

"You and your friends are the upper crust," she sometimes remarked. "I'm just a middle-class girl, barely, from Southern Ohio."

"You're wonderful. You're beautiful—I don't care where you're from!" Austin would always try to reassure his naturally glamorous, poised, yet inexplicably insecure wife.

Everyone who was the least bit interested in the up-and-coming symphony in Southwest Florida's crown-jewel community was in attendance, at least those with some measure of interest and a better measure of money.

People in Naples who were wealthy, many of them transplants, were there, seeing and being seen, though not wanting to be obvious about either. The affluent had achieved a level of success that brought with it some degree of projected indifference, busy people, many of them overscheduled, who chose the fund-raiser over one or two other invitations or commitments. Many had planned to arrive late and leave early.

"I'm sorry, dear. We have another engagement tonight, and we really must put in an appearance. I do hope we can see each other again soon. Please call me your first chance—" or some version of this was heard occasionally within the polite crowd.

This was the typical tone of patrons that night; some warm, some pretentious, but the conveyance of importance was consistent; important lives, important thinking, and important places to go.

Except for Austin and Angela Morris, they were the darlings of the throng, the unpretentious, obviously in-love-with-each-other couple. Neither was aloof, indifferent, nor distractible when talking with their fellow Naples residents and part-time residents. Austin and Angela listened when others talked, and they asked questions that reflected their interest and empathy.

"But, Joan, what are you and Fredrik going to do if Fredrik sells his company?" Angela was asking Joan Werner almost at the same time Austin was asking a similar question to Fredrik on the other side of the ballroom.

"Are you going to start something new—like a new company or a new career?" Austin had asked.

But before Fredrik could answer, he was interrupted by his wife Joan, saying, "Honey, here's someone you simply must meet."

Joan was excited about her new friend Angela whom she had met at the Bay Colony Golf Club, standing in line for a grilled chopped sirloin burger, some six weeks earlier.

Joan and Fredrik had recently purchased a home in the Bay Colony section of Pelican Marsh, and it was Joan's intent to meet as many of the neighbors as possible, although many of them were at home very sporadically. Like she and Fredrik, most of Bay Colony's residents had at least one home elsewhere that vied for their time and attention. And all Bay Colony's elite traveled extensively.

"Are you new here?" Joan had asked the beautiful, dark-haired golfer in front of her. She was very pleased and very surprised when the slender, perfect-bodied lady who looked considerably younger than she turned and, with a broad, warm smile, responded, "No, but I felt like it on the back nine today. Hi, I'm Angela Morris."

"And I'm Joan Werner. We live over on Dormie Drive. And you?"

"My husband Austin and I and our baby daughter Samantha live north of here in Mediterra, off Livingston."

The two had clicked immediately. Joan was basically a down-to-earth Midwesterner as was Angela. Joan had met Fredrik in college at Ohio University, she a young girl from the town of Athens, Ohio, and he an out-of-state student from the Pittsburgh area. Even back then, Joan was the secretly shy but outgoing "social butterfly," introducing herself and making friends wherever she went.

She said very little about her husband to sorority sisters or, later on, to social friends. She knew he was stiff, something of a social bore, but he was always adoring and supportive of her. He was logical, structured, and somewhat cold like his German immigrant parents. His father had been a chemical engineer at U.S. Steel and his mother a high school math teacher, whose English, which all the kids had complained, was extremely difficult to understand.

Joan and Angela had arranged to play golf soon after they met and had a wonderful time together. Each had felt very relaxed and able to be herself. It had been a perfect day.

So Joan was delighted to have the opportunity to introduce her new friend, perhaps with the potential of becoming her best friend, to her husband.

She had told Fredrik about her sleek and athletic friend Angela. "When you meet her, I'm going to have to watch you so you don't use your smooth Germanic charm to hit on her," she had kidded, always trying to "loosen him up."

"Not to worry, darling," the generally unsmiling, always proper Fredrik had reassured, not recognizing the jocular nature of her comment. "No woman could ever cause my eye to roam from you!"

Joan mostly loved her husband, although there were times when she wished other people could see his big heart, his humanism as she did. Perhaps because of the way he was raised and the way he had worked so hard to build a business that was now being wooed by acquisition-hungry suitors, Fredrik Werner never seemed to let down his guard with anyone but Joan.

Joan and Angela approached the two men at the punch bowl, one facing them and one with his back to them, waiting for his cup to be filled by the server in the stiffly starched jacket.

The confident, relaxed man facing them with the brilliantly white smile must be Angela's husband, Joan thought. Clearly, the bulky, wide-shouldered gentleman with the crew cut about to turn around was Fredrik. He had

3

heard Joan alerting him that she had yet another person for him to meet just as he was starting to respond to Austin Morris's question and exerting care not to spill the cup handed to him by the starched jacket.

As Fredrik wheeled around, his eyes met Angela's before they connected with Joan's. Never illogical and rarely spontaneous, the multimillionaire blurted out with an accent traceable back to his parents' province of Heidenheim, "Marie, is that you?"

CHAPTER 2

Angela Morris flushed, tried to mask her humiliation and discomfort, and reacted with all the casualness she could muster. "Pardon me? No, my name is *Angela*. Angela Morris."

Joan rushed into the gap, saying, "You know, Fredrik, I've told you about Angela—she's my new very good friend. She lives in Mediterranean and is an excellent golfer."

"And I'm Angela's husband Austin. You must be Joan." The confident man had lost some of his poise, but no one seemed to notice.

Joan was so pleased, so nearly exuberant that she had found a woman with a nice husband whom Fredrik seemed to like. The two men had been talking for quite a while, she had observed.

Socializing and building a social life was not easy. Joan wanted to be social, to gain acceptance in this society she and her husband had become part of, but Fredrik didn't seem particularly interested. So many times she and Fredrik had met another couple, had tried to build a friendship, but efforts (mostly hers) had quietly fizzled. Both the other husband and wife had liked Joan, but they didn't care much for Fredrik; too straitlaced, too serious, and not much fun.

Perhaps this time, things would be different. She was so hopeful, she readily forgot Fredrik's calling Angela by the wrong name. It was not unusual for Fredrik to make some sort of faux pas.

But the three other folks did not forget. Austin, being the kind, considerate, mostly forgiving gentleman that he was, did not want to make an issue out of it. In fact, he did not even mention it to Angela that night as she laid her head on his shoulder while the limo sped north on

Livingston toward their majestic home in Mediterra. He wasn't sure if he would ever mention it.

Angela was desperately trying to cover her fear, which felt like terror, as she thought about the awkward moment she was called Marie. She hadn't been called that in a long time, another lifetime ago in fact. She prayed to God that Austin hadn't quite heard it.

Please, God, don't let Austin find out about me, about my past. I've changed, you know that! I never wanted to live my past life the way I did. I promised that if I could ever escape that life, I would never go back. Please, God, let me keep what I have. Let me be forgiven!

* * *

Fredrik's steel-trap mind was very sharp. He never forgot a face and rarely forgot a name, particularly if the two belonged to a beautiful woman and especially if the beautiful woman was one with whom he had gone to bed. This was one time he was glad his wife Joan was not especially detailed; she may have perceived that he had called her new friend Marie, but she would forget.

CHAPTER 3

Austin slept very little that night. He was concerned, even worried, about what his new acquaintance Fredrik had called Angela at the event. Marie was, in fact, Angela's middle name, but he had never known her to be called by that name.

"I hate my middle name," Angela had told him emphatically.

Austin was reluctant to bring up the incident, at least for now. He loved the stable family life he and Angela had created together. And he absolutely adored their little girl Samantha. He vowed when he first held her in the delivery room that he would never do anything to disrupt her life or create traumas for her.

"Here's our gift from God!" he had proclaimed to the groggy but ecstatic Angela.

Austin lay in bed, staring toward the dark, cavernous vaulted ceiling of their master bedroom. He sensed that Angela too was awake, but she didn't move and was breathing with seemingly easy regularity.

No, this is not the time to bring up this business about Fredrik Werner calling her Marie, he thought to himself. Things were going so well for the three of them, and besides, he thought he could only handle so many things at one time. He had learned from his first wife, Lorena, that it was best to pace oneself, to take things in sequence or in stride. She had also taught him about the enduring qualities of love and that everyone has some private aspects to their lives.

"To try to know everything about someone, even if you love that person, can become invasive, even possessive. Sometimes we need to be satisfied with what we have for the moment or the unforeseeable future."

Austin was more than curious and even had anxiety around Angela being referred to as Marie. But again, he could only handle so many things at one time. Maybe it was a name her longtime boyfriend in high school and college, Kenny Chessin, had called her, and somehow the name got passed on to Fredrik Werner. It was too bad he couldn't contact Kenny to find out if some way or another, Kenny had known Fredrik and referred to his girlfriend as Marie. Austin thought maybe he could get to know Fredrik better in the next few weeks and ask him if he had ever known a guy named Kenny Chessin. All in the proper sequence . . .

His mind went back to earlier that same day when his attorney, Allan Federer, had called.

"I have some disturbing news, Austin. I have had a couple of telephone conversations with a Ms. Rosen, Janie Rosen, who lives in Beachwood, Ohio, and Boca Raton. She wants to schedule a meeting with you to talk about your first wife, Lorena."

"What—what about Lorena?" Austin was caught somewhat off guard and always had pangs of emptiness whenever Lorena's name or memory abruptly came into his consciousness. He would always miss her.

"Ms. Rosen thinks that her mother, Elinor Rosen, knew Lorena way back when. Elinor now spends all her time in Boca, part of the time at a nursing home. She has Alzheimer's, and her daughter Janie spends almost half her time in Boca."

"Why doesn't she move to Boca?" Austin wondered why he wanted to know.

"Janie is a therapist or counselor. She's a social worker who has a private practice in Cleveland, recently got licensed in Florida, and is trying to sell her practice in Cleveland so she can move to Boca Raton full time." Allan Federer always had the answers.

"I don't understand . . . What does she want from me? And why didn't she just contact me directly?" Austin asked with a sound of skepticism in his voice.

"I think she wants money—who doesn't?" Allan said in a clipped, serious way. "She said she has been doing research about you and the company and found my name as executive vice president and general counsel. She said she wants to keep everything businesslike and professional."

"So what does that mean?" Austin asked as if he were wondering to himself out loud.

"I think it means she was afraid to approach you directly . . ."

"But why? Why wouldn't she just pick up the phone and call me directly?" Austin continued to feel puzzled.

"Maybe she was afraid, and maybe she wasn't. Maybe she is intimidated by your president's title. I think she felt a little bit of trust, a little bit of a connection with me."

"How come?"

"Because in her research on me, she learned that I have a cousin named Fran, who is also from Beachwood and Shaker Heights. Fran is actually her aunt."

"Well, what do you think I should do, Allan?" Austin was anxious and still somewhat confused. What did this woman want? Allan thought she wanted money, but Austin had a very odd feeling that she wanted something more than money.

CHAPTER 4

In the waning hours of darkness, Austin drifted into a light sleep. Having resolved that for the time being, he would not bring up the encounter with Fredrik Werner with Angela, not until he found out what this Rosen woman wanted.

Angela never had the good fortune of falling asleep. She knew Austin was awake for a long time, probably mulling over and over the Fredrik Werner exchange.

She hoped Austin would never ask about it, never bring it up. If he did, she had no idea how she would handle it.

She could tell the truth, or she could lie. Maybe she could tell some of the truth but hide parts of it. Austin already knew quite a bit about Kenny, who had been her first and only real boyfriend, but Austin didn't know the kind of hold Kenny had had over her. Nor did he know the kinds of things Kenny had expected her to do.

Angela totally loved Austin. He had been a savior, having helped her start over with a new life. He knew he had helped her improve her life—he just didn't know how bad it had been or how deeply the shame from her life before him permeated her soul.

Angela finally decided that if Austin asked her about why someone had called her Marie, she would tell him part of the truth. She would hide those pieces of the past that could be most damaging to Samantha and to their three lives together as a family.

PART II

CHAPTER 5

Angela Marie Capelli was born in Appalachia, along the Ohio River in Gallipolis, Ohio. Her parents had mixed feelings about having a baby as neither was certain they could afford a third mouth to feed. Once her mom held little Angela, she knew she would find a way to support her and possibly give her some of the things she had never had.

Angela's father worked on a riverboat that transported barges, mostly filled with coal, down the Ohio River to the Mississippi. His typical work pattern of thirty days on and thirty days off tragically ended when he fell from one of the barges into the river, likely destroyed by the propellers of the giant diesel engines.

Angela's mom, pregnant with Angela's soon-to-be sister Katherine, sank into a deep hole of depression, and began to reverse roles with her six-year-old firstborn.

"Mommy doesn't feel good . . . Can you be an angel and fix your own dinner tonight?"

Later on, "Could you be Mommy's little helper and change the baby's diaper? And see if you can be a big girl and get her bottle ready."

Angela always obliged and always tried to do whatever her mom asked her to do. She did her homework when she could get to it, with cooking and junior-mommy work being top priorities.

She missed her dad so much. She lay in bed at night and remembered his strong, black-haired arms lifting her high and hugging her. "Daddy's little princess, that's what you are! No matter how many kids I have, you will always be my number one!"

She cried and muffled the noise. She did not want her mom to hear because it would just make her sadder. Mommy had lost her husband and was now what they call a widow, like a spider or something. Angela did not want to be a burden to her mom or cause her to feel any worse than she already did.

Angela Marie was a beautiful young girl with dark hair, dark eyes, and a dazzling smile. Her flashing eyes and friendliness conveyed to others that she was cheerful, always in a good mood, and fundamentally a happy, normal child.

But beneath her outward persona was sadness, a worrisome inner world of fear and dread, fear that she would never have a future with fun and opportunities and dread that her mom's life would end as abruptly and tragically as her dad's had ended.

"Mommy, you really need to be more careful. Last night, after Katherine and I went to bed, I heard you fall against the kitchen table. I was afraid to get up out of bed, afraid you would be mad at me. Did you have another dizzy spell?"

By now, the serious-for-her-ten-years Angela knew the spells were brought on by alcohol consumption, frequent and heavy consumption. She knew her mom had been something of a drinker for a long time. With some self-prodding, she could remember good moods and loud laughter spiraling into angry shouting and arguing, back when her dad was still alive.

Both her parents had looked forward to his thirty days off and were primed to party when he came into the house from the shipyard. Sometimes they would stay up all night the first night he came home, drinking, talking, and playing Italian opera music loudly.

Angela's father was Italian, his own father having come directly from the old country in time to enter first grade at Gallipolis City Schools. This grandfather, whom Angela never knew, began school, unable to speak a word of English. But he got by; he did okay as some of the students befriended him and helped him learn.

Angela's father told the story more than once, of what a great country America was and what a special community Gallipolis was. "My dad couldn't speak a lick of English, but the people here accepted him anyway and took him under their wing. We owe a lot to the people here. I'm just sorry Papa never lived long enough to enjoy his golden years with the people he grew up with."

Very unfortunately, Mr. Capelli Sr., Angela's grandfather, was driving home from the clothing store on Second Avenue where he worked as a clerk during the day and a tailor at night. It had been just after Thanksgiving, and the Christmas rush was beginning, even in Gallipolis. Mr. Capelli had sold three suits that day and had worked late into the night, trying to complete what were extensive alterations.

As he drove by Miletti's, a run-down little bar at the lower end of town, he thought momentarily about stopping in to have a quick beer and maybe a hot dog. Miletti's hot dogs were famous for their chili sauce, and people came several miles to eat the chili dogs and take a pint or even a quart of the spicy condiment home.

Mr. Capelli Sr. hesitated, started to slow down to turn right into Miletti's cramped little parking lot but looked at his watch and saw it was eleven thirty, and slowly reaccelerated.

In a flash, his life was gone. A young man named Jimmy Bateman, fairly inebriated, was leaving the parking lot, saw the lumbering old station wagon slow down, and then gunned his engine to launch onto Garfield Street. In a sickening split second, Jimmy realized the station wagon was not going to pull in but, instead, was going to continue southward toward Lower River Road.

Jimmy's hot Camaro broadsided Mr. Capelli's Buick, pushing it head-on into a pickup truck operated by Marvin Wheeler. The stars were horribly misaligned that December night, and neither Mr. Capelli nor Mr. Wheeler ever knew what hit them. They were pronounced dead at the scene by the emergency medical team from Holzer Hospital.

Jimmy Bateman was unscratched and unhurt physically, but he never recovered from the trauma of that night. He was completely cooperative, sobbing, and agreed to be tested for his blood-alcohol content. "I did it. I'm guilty. I know I'm a DUI! I don't feel drunk, but I know I am!" he confessed between hysterical outcries. The police officer on duty cited him for reckless operation and for driving under the influence of alcohol.

Mr. Capelli Sr.'s life ended prematurely and tragically with alcohol being a major contributing factor. Two years later, when Angela's father's life ended in the Ohio River, it was strongly rumored that alcohol was a big factor, that he had been drunk when he fell.

Angela was twelve when she heard that rumor.

CHAPTER 6

Junior high school in Gallipolis was hard work for Angela. Her mother continued in a cycle of depression, binge drinking, brief periods of euphoria, and then anger. The anger seemed directed at her deceased husband, at God, and at life in general. Sometimes she even got angry at her girls.

Angela, who—by almost anyone's standards—was a very dedicated, hardworking daughter at age fourteen, began working at the same clothing store where her grandfather Capelli had worked. She rode her bike to run errands, take packages up Second Avenue to mail at the post office, and then pick up food and snacks for the clerks, the assistant manager, and the manager. She also cleaned the store three nights a week and rearranged the window displays at least once a month.

"Louie's granddaughter has style. She has taste. She has an eye for what goes together and catches people's attention as they look in the window," the store manager told his best salesperson and assistant manager, Kenny Chessin.

"Yeah, and she's mighty easy on the eyes too," the twenty-one-year-old hotshot salesman and assistant manager retorted. Kenny was smooth and confident and hoped his part-time college career nearby at the University of Rio Grande would one day lead him to becoming a high school teacher or guidance counselor.

"You're a dirty old man, and you're barely old enough to drink," the manager reacted with feigned disapproval.

"When they're old enough to sprout, they're old enough to sample," Kenny leered, rolling his eyes. He tried to never let Angela know or be aware of his staring at her, imagining what she looked like naked, and vowing to himself that he would be the first man to show her what sex was all about.

"Well, let me know how the sampling goes, stud," the manager said, and both men laughed loudly as if they had just see a funny pornographic scene.

Angela sensed that the cool, convertible-driving Kenny watched her whenever he thought he could do so without being noticed. She wasn't sure about this man-woman thing, although she had read some pamphlets that had been passed out without explanation in eighth-grade health class. The pictures had shown diagrams of a man's penis and a woman's vagina, but no one had the nerve to ask questions.

Some of the athletes in high school asked her out, but she was basically afraid. She was afraid they might try to touch her breasts or try to get her to touch them. Her friend Sally, whose father was a minister, told her that sex was bad and was dirty unless a husband and wife did it together in an attempt to have children. Apparently, they could only have sex if they were trying to make a baby. But just exactly how the penis and vagina got together and created a pregnancy was not clear. Somehow, an egg got fertilized and became an embryo, a future person.

It didn't seem like sex would be fun, but she guessed she would eventually find out. Her mom never dated after her dad died, and Angela didn't have time for dating. Her mom, though, actually encouraged her to go out with boys. "Why don't you go to the movies with Tom Fleming? His dad's a doctor, so you know Tom will have money someday."

Usually, Angela's mom would go on to say, "You have to marry for money, Angie. Long after the love and the sex are gone, the money will still be there."

No, this sex business didn't sound like much fun, but maybe if the man had money, it would help take one's mind off the sex.

CHAPTER 7

"Let me take you to dinner to celebrate your sweet-sixteen birthday!" Kenny implored, having been trying to butter up Angela and helping her overcome her shyness for almost two years now.

"I don't know, Kenny. If my mom ever finds out—"

"You can bring her with you," Kenny lied, knowing that Angela would never want her run-down, overweight alcoholic mom to come with them. He actually sensed that the idea of going out on her sixteenth birthday with a dapper, successful man about town who also went to college had some intrigue, some appeal to the very striking, sexy without trying to be sexy teenager.

"She's jailbait," Carl, the manager, had told Kenny privately when he heard Kenny coming on to Angela.

"Yeah, but what a way to go to the slammer," Kenny would react, rolling his eyes as though he were dreaming.

Kenny secretly had it figured out that if he could start taking her out, be her friend—like a brother—and eventually become her confidante, he could start teaching her about sexual favors and how to pleasure a man. No rush; he saw her as his long-term project. "Project Virgin" was how he thought of Angela in his mind.

One giant lever Kenny knew he could use with Angela was money. He had already trained her to accept small tips—$2 here, $4 there—for running errands and picking up food for him. Kenny knew he wasn't rich, but he also knew that to Angela, he was.

And he knew she was poor. All the money she made at the store seemed to go for supporting her mother and her sister. Her sister seemed to be slow, maybe even retarded, but Kenny never asked. He sensed that

Angela didn't want to talk about her sister or her mom. Maybe she was ashamed of them; Kenny could see why.

Kenny's heart pounded, and he felt a swelling in his silk boxers as Angela came into the store on that incredible Saturday that was her sixteenth birthday. She was all dressed up in a simple black dress with black flats. She was wearing a slightly tinted hose and had her hair pulled back with a black velvet ribbon. Her makeup was understated and perfect.

"Well?" Kenny asked, nervously begging God for the answer he received.

"I've decided you can take me out tonight," the most popular girl of his fantasy life said as she sparkled.

CHAPTER 8

"Oh, Kenny! Tonight was wonderful! It all went so fast!" the thoroughly appreciative Angela exclaimed to Kenny.

Kenny had spared no expense in taking Angela to Point Pleasant, West Virginia, across the Ohio River from Gallipolis, to the Point Grille, reputedly the best restaurant in the tri-county area.

"I hope you don't mind if I get a steak, Kenny," Angela's eyes had shone as she sought his permission.

"Whatever you want, princess! This is your sixteenth birthday, and I want you to get exactly what you want. You're worth it and then some!" Kenny felt the eyes staring at the remarkably striking young lady he was escorting. He knew if they had been in Hollywood, the restaurant patrons would have felt certain she was an up-and-coming star.

"Is this one a good one?" Her eyes and voice had reflected innocence as she pointed to the filet mignon on the menu.

"That would be the best—my choice too." Kenny tried to convey that he fully endorsed her selection. He wanted to treat her as a very special, extraordinary person. He would respect her fragile young psyche and never do anything to hurt her. He saw her as his princess, his china doll, and his long-term prize.

As they left the Point Grille, they were both full, she even a bit stuffed, and the evening air made her legs feel rubbery.

"Oh, Kenny. I feel wobbly," she said honestly, and Kenny immediately put his arm around her to provide support.

"Don't worry, princess, you can relax in the car and listen to your favorite music as we head back to Ohio. What time do you need to be home?"

"Kenny, I don't want to go home! I don't want this evening to end. I don't want my birthday to end."

He opened the door for her, helped her get settled in the car, and then went around the front of the car to his door, never taking his eyes off the sixteen-year-old he adored. He smoothly slid into the driver's seat and asked, "Would you like to put the top down again?"

"Oh yes! I'll do it. I can do it!" she reacted with youthful enthusiasm. She loved the way Kenny treated her as if she were an adult and encouraged her to do whatever she wanted to do. He never tried to force her to do anything she didn't want to do and always responded to her as if she were the most important person in his world.

"Princess, open the glove compartment."

"Okay!" Her enthusiasm became excitement when she saw a small pale-yellow box with a hand-tied red bow on top. She recognized the signature wrapping of Bailey's, the finest jewelry store in Gallipolis.

"Oh my gosh, Kenny. What are you doing?"

"I'm giving you a present, a birthday present! I'm giving you something to remember this birthday by so you'll never forget it."

"My gosh, Kenny. You treat me like a queen—a princess I mean. Why do you like me—"

Angela was going to complete the question with the words *so much*, but the untaped yellow wrapping paper fell open, revealing the important, expensive-looking ruby-red box from Bailey's. She opened it without delay and began to gasp and cry.

"Kenny! Oh, Kenny!" She awkwardly reached over and tried to hug his broad-shouldered frame.

"C'mon. Try it on," Kenny encouraged, he himself fighting to keep the tears and his own excitement from showing.

After completing the hug and kissing him wetly on the cheek, Angela, without embarrassment, said, "Oh, please, Kenny. Help me."

Kenny not so deftly scooped the sterling silver chain with the tiny diamond-veneered "A" pendant from its ruby home and asked Angela to turn and face away from him.

"I'm not very good at this, but I'll try," Kenny said as his big thumbs and fingers separated the clasp and reached over her head to pull the ends of the necklace together. Angela held her black hair up in her back, revealing a pure, sculpted neck that Kenny agonizingly refrained from kissing. Luckily, he fastened the clasp on the first try.

"Oh, let me see it, Kenny!" Angela exclaimed with delight as she eagerly pulled the car's rearview mirror toward her.

It was still light enough on the warm midsummer evening for her to gasp again as she caught the glamour of the sparkling "A" looking back at her.

"Thank you! Thank you!" she kept saying as she hugged Kenny again. "This is the best birthday I've ever had and probably ever will have!"

She was crying when she kissed him again—this time, wetly on the mouth.

CHAPTER 9

Kenny was in love with Angela. Two years had passed since their first date on her sixteenth birthday, and he had been relentless in his pursuit of her companionship and affection. He had watched over her like a protective uncle, not wanting another man—and certainly not a boy—to come into the picture as a competitor, no, more as an intruder.

"I hope you never fall for some of those high school yo-yos," he said playfully to the nicely developed eighteen-year-old Angela. He loved her medium-sized and perky breasts, which she had let him touch and kiss after he had successfully coaxed her to bare them.

"But, Kenny, I'm not sure I should be doing this," she had protested the first time, with small baby tears coming from her sad dark eyes.

"With me, it's okay. You know I will never hurt you. I love you, princess, and I will always take care of you. It's the other guys you need to worry about. They want to use you, have sex with you, and then move on. They will leave you, and may God strike me dead, I never will!"

"But you want to have sex with me too, Kenny." She found all this touching and fondling sort of nice but scary.

"No, I don't. I want to *make love* with you. There's a huge difference between having sex and making love. Sex is one-sided, but making love is mutual."

"But I don't know if I want to do either one," she said, the tears now dried as she lay back in the front seat of Kenny's convertible, her blouse and bra in the small compartment behind the seats.

The brand-new sports car's top had also been removed and was neatly tucked out of sight beneath a fiberglass panel that extended forward from where a regular car's trunk would have been.

Kenny's head was softly, lightly planted against her chest, somewhat on her left breast, staring at her right breast.

"What are you doing, Kenny?" she asked but knew the answer.

"I'm just watching your pretty little right nipple stand up," he responded with fascination as he watched it enlarge when he gently used his left index finger to play with it.

"Oh, Kenny. I want to make love to you—I want you to be the first!"

"Let's make sure we're both ready," he said with considerable restraint. For at least two years now, he had imagined consummating the act with Angela when she turned eighteen. They had come close a few times, but it was usually him who had backed away.

"I want it to be so special, so intense and enjoyable that you never forget it," he said to reassure her and to reinforce his own thinking.

"Oh, I won't forget. I know I won't! I promise, Kenny!" Angela felt that Kenny more than deserved whatever she could give him. He had shown her a number of good times and had taken extremely good care of her for over two years in high school. At first, he had taken her wherever she wanted to go, then had taught her to drive, and then had given her a car. He had freely given her money, lots of it, which had enabled her, her mother, and her sister to live very comfortably. He made more money than she could imagine now that he was a manager of a men's clothing store.

"You are unbelievable—I will never forget you, no matter what!" Angela repeated the sentiment, partly because she thought Kenny really wanted to hear it at times like this. He seemed a little bit afraid that she would meet someone, instantly fall in love, and then leave him.

Angela really meant what she said because no one other than her dad, whom she vividly remembered, had ever made her feel safe the way Kenny did. She always felt her dad was strong, would protect her, and would do anything for her. She had had inexplicable feelings of being safe and secure when he was home in spite of some of the drinking and arguing that went on and that actually increased over time.

"I feel safe with you, darling." She still felt a bit awkward or self-conscious calling him anything but Kenny as if she were following a script for the first time. But she knew he liked it and did not perceive her self-consciousness. "You make me feel the same way I did when my dad was alive—you are my big strong protector."

"You're right, princess—nothing bad is ever going to happen to you as long as I live and you keep me in your life."

"I will. I will, Kenny! Forever!" She held his head tight against her bosom and knew that he was aroused. "What about tonight, Kenny? Should we?"

"No, I want to, but I'm going to pleasure you and then let you pleasure me. We're going to save the lovemaking till Christmas. We're going to go away someplace you'll never forget, and we're going to go all the way. We're going to make love, and you're never going to make love with anyone else again. You may have sex with other men, but you won't make love."

CHAPTER 10

This differentiating of sex and love was always confusing for Angela. Love seemed to be how a person felt about another person, and sex seemed to be an activity that led to physical pleasure and maybe even babies. Not that she wanted babies, but her friend Sally had always said that to have sex just for pleasure was wrong, that it was the temptation and lure of the devil.

"But how can making love with Kenny be so wrong? He's taken care of me and my family. Without him, I'd probably be a high school dropout, maybe even pregnant. I know I wouldn't have been able to continue living with my mom and her alcohol problem if it hadn't been for Kenny."

"But you don't really know that. You've let Kenny support you financially and provide enough money so that your mom can hide her problem behind an outward façade of respectability," her staunch Christian friend Sally had asserted.

"But I know if we didn't have money, thanks to Kenny, we'd be broke, probably out on the street, and Mom and my sister and I would be looking for our next homeless shelter."

"Maybe and maybe not. You never know what might happen, what might have been if Kenny hadn't given you the money, the car, and the security for your family. But I think you've paid a price for all that, don't you?" Sally asked with the sense of righteousness and barely harnessed zeal of a missionary.

"What do you mean?" Angela countered.

"You've given up two and a half of the best years of your life, a big part of your high school. You haven't dated. You're a recluse in school. You don't really know any of the guys. You're seen as this beautiful girl who's almost possessed by some older guy who supports you. Everybody thinks you've been sleeping with him for years and predicts you'll be pregnant by the time you graduate."

"Well, maybe I will be . . . but only if I can get Kenny to screw me. No offense, Sally, but please try not to judge me. I admit I don't know everything I'm doing, but I think I've done pretty well. My mom, my sister, and I are not street people, and we all get along okay. My sister is getting special education, some special training that will help her work at some kind of trade, doing manual work.

"And she will be self-sufficient," Angela continued. "She won't be on welfare, and she'll have a good life. She'll be able to live up to her potential, be happy, and maybe someday, get married."

"But this could happen with or without Kenny," Sally intervened, prepared to talk about the power of faith and belief in God.

"You may be right, Sally," Angela partially conceded. "But I'm not smart enough to figure it all out or confident enough to give up what I've got. Kenny and I have plans after I graduate. He says that we may move or that I may move and he'll stay here. A lot depends on whether he gets a good job as a teacher or guidance counselor and if he can afford to leave the manager's job at the store.

"He says he has some friends at Ohio University where I want to go to college. They can get me set up and help me make a lot of money."

"A lot of money doing what?" Sally asked in a tone more demanding than even Angela's mother used.

"I'm not sure . . . I think it's some kind of modeling or escort service or something like that."

Sally looked as if she had been punched in the gut. "No, Angela. Don't do it. Kenny is going to lead you down some path that you'll regret. Money or no money, you can't sell yourself like some prostitute!"

"I won't be any kind of prostitute, Sally," Angela said, now determined to reassure her good but judgmental friend. "Kenny would never make me do anything I didn't want to do," she said with certainty, reflecting on the most recent time she had wanted him to make love to her but he had declined.

CHAPTER 11

It was the day after Christmas, and Kenny and Angela boarded the huge jet aircraft at Columbus International Airport. They had left Gallipolis at six thirty in the morning, allowing plenty of time to stop along the way for breakfast.

"Oh, darling, I've never been to Las Vegas! I'm so excited I could just explode! I'm not hungry—I don't want anything that might get my stomach upset."

"But you've never gotten sick when we've flown to Florida," the lovestruck Kenny reminded her. "We've been there three times now, and you've never had to use one of those air sickness bags."

"You mean barf bags, don't you?" the beautiful, growing-in-confidence young Angela laughed naturally.

Kenny laughed with her; he loved her upbeat, good-natured humor. She was cute—no, more than cute. She was everything he could ever dream for and probably more than he deserved.

He wanted to possess her, to control her, but he knew that any obvious attempts to do so might frighten her away. It scared him to no end to imagine her falling in love with some other guy and ultimately leaving him. He knew he would kill any man who took her away from him.

"You're too much, princess."

"What do you mean?"

"You're too good to be true. I don't really deserve you, and I start getting paranoid when I think about how any guy on the planet would want you for his girlfriend . . . How did I get you?" he asked with amazement that never quite went away.

28

"Well, it wasn't just that you got me—I got you too. You've always said love is mutual, that it takes two to make love."

"Yeah, but I still think I'm the lucky one in this equation," Kenny said with all honesty. "I wish they offered more psychology courses at Rio Grande. I would have taken them to figure out why I'm so paranoid about losing you."

"Don't worry about it, Kenny. Please don't. I'm never going to leave you. Now that you finally broke down and gave me what I wanted—what you made me beg for—I could never walk away."

That summer, on her eighteenth birthday, she had finally enticed Kenny to do what they had both thought about incessantly and had wanted to do—make love. It had been pretty much as they both had imagined, very nerve-racking but loving, and very considerate of the other person.

Afterward, they both had felt guilty and had lain back on Kenny's bed, not knowing what to say.

"Do you feel guilty?" Kenny had finally asked.

"No, not really . . . well, maybe a little," Angela had answered tentatively.

"I'm sorry, princess. I swore I would never be the one to hurt you or make you feel bad." Kenny tried to be supportive but also started to cry.

"Maybe you can help me get over it," she said with eyes that hypnotized.

"I want to. I will," he said.

"Then let's do it again," the most beautiful girl in Gallipolis said as she rolled on top of him.

Chapter 12

Las Vegas was hot that December, but locals insisted to the lovebirds from Ohio that it was unseasonably warm. Angela and Kenny didn't mind because the air felt crisp and warmly reassuring when they thought about the cold, damp air they had left behind.

"What are we going to do for a whole four days in Las Vegas?" Angela had asked during the flight.

"Make love, gamble, eat, and make love some more," Kenny had answered spontaneously.

"Maybe we won't need to do all that gambling and eating," Angela said in a voice that sounded seductive as she reached beneath the first-class-provided blanket on Kenny's lap.

He responded immediately and told her that he loved her.

"I never thought I could love someone the way I love you, princess. I want to be with you all the time. I worry all the time that something bad might happen to you. I want to take care of you and to make sure no man ever makes love to you."

"Don't worry, darling. You're the only man who ever will."

"It might be good for a man to have sex with you in case I don't satisfy you completely," Kenny said in a tone that was somewhat unnerving to Angela. She didn't want to disagree with him to make him feel insecure, but it didn't make sense to her. He seemed to contradict himself.

"I don't want to have sex with another man, make love with another man, or even be with another man," she said with a note of finality, hoping to close off this conversation topic.

But Kenny continued, "My friends in Columbus have connections that could lead to a lot of money. When you go to college at Ohio State, you can work occasional weekends, entertaining important businessmen who want to be seen with a beautiful coed like you."

"But, Kenny, I thought I was going to go to Ohio University in Athens—"

"I've changed—I mean we've changed our minds. That is, unless you want to be in Athens while I'm in Columbus."

"Wait a minute, Kenny—did you get the teaching job in Columbus?"

"I did—you're looking at and touching a brand-new high school English teacher in Columbus City Schools!"

"Oh, Kenny! Congratulations! Does this mean we're going to move to Columbus together? Soon?"

"It sure does, baby!" Kenny was feeling some energy, some confidence flow back into his body. He had been worried that she might reject out of hand the mention of entertaining businessmen. But he had been much more worried that she might hang onto the idea of going to Ohio University, even after finding out he was going to be moving to Columbus.

Angela looked longingly at her rugged-looking tall hero. He really loved her, she told herself. He certainly had taken good care of her and her family. Making money to help repay him seemed reasonable, although she wasn't sure about the idea of escorting or entertaining men. And it was very confusing that Kenny would make mention of her possibly even having sex with them.

He didn't seem like what she imagined a pimp to be, but maybe Sally was right. Maybe Kenny would lead her down some wicked path. But Angela knew Kenny would never force her to do something she didn't want to do.

Maybe the businessmen would be older and just want to use someone like her as a status symbol: "Look at me—I may not be young, but this young girl with me is evidence I am still strong and virile."

CHAPTER 13

"I don't know, Kenny," Angela said in the darkness as they lay naked in the luxurious king-size bed. It was only their first night in Las Vegas, and they had made love, gambled, and eaten.

"Don't know what?" Kenny reacted immediately, hoping his voice didn't sound panicky.

"This idea of going out with businessmen. I would only do something like that if you really wanted me to. You said, though, that you're almost paranoid about me finding someone. Wouldn't my entertaining businessmen make all that worse?" she asked, hoping he would say yes or maybe.

"No, I don't think so. You would be doing it for me, not because you wanted to be with other men. We could make a lot of money, and any physical involvement would just be sex, not love. Most of these guys probably just want to look the part, to be seen with a beautiful, classy, young girl. You might have a little sex from time to time, but it would be for *us*. You would save all your love for me."

Kenny wasn't real sure this made sense to him, let alone to Angela. He just knew that he had some kind of desire to control Angela, to *own* her. It was becoming a fantasy to him that when they made love, he imagined she was having sex with another man but thinking of him. He wanted her to think only of him and to regard other men as nothing, as people without human feelings whom she could use to make money.

He never talked about these feelings, but he worried that they were weird. He would be afraid to discuss them with a counselor, although he had been told he could use a good shrink, mainly by fellow students at Rio Grande who thought he had something of a death wish or self-destructive bent.

"The way you drive your Corvette ninety to a hundred miles per hour and the way you blatantly sell drugs on campus, you know you're flirting with danger," his buddy Roger Eagleston had told him several times.

"You've got it made, and you don't even know it or appreciate it. You've got a gorgeous, totally devoted high school girlfriend, a new 'Vette, a good job, and a career that could go several positive directions. But you risk it all every day. Maybe you don't feel you deserve what you've got," Roger had continued.

CHAPTER 14

Angela was beginning to understand the difference between sex and making love. As a first-year student at Ohio State University (OSU), it was clear that most of the boys were interested in one thing when it came to members of the opposite sex: seeing how quickly they could get them into bed.

"Men see sex as a conquest. Women see sex as a commitment," the professor had told the "psychology of adjustment" class. The quirky old scholar who was nicknamed Einstein because of his appearance liked to explain his views and personal opinions on sex to the class and watch the young women to see who was wide-eyed and naïve and who was mostly in agreement.

The most striking coed in the classroom, Ms. Capelli, was neither. She seemed to be listening but not affected. She seemed to be very serious and wanted to take notes and learn in order to get a good grade.

Leaving Gallipolis to move to Columbus had been painful for Angela—much more painful than she had thought it would be. Her mom and sister had cried with surprising intensity, but Angela could read between the lines of their tears that they both thought she was doing the right thing.

They both thought Kenny was a great choice for Angela and for the Capelli family. Clearly, Kenny thought the world of Angela, and he had lots of money that he generously shared with both of them.

"Don't ever let that Kenny get away, Angie. He's a wonderful catch, a real keeper," her mom didn't mind telling her.

"That sounds like he's a big fish, Mom, like I hooked him and I need to do whatever I have to do to keep him from getting away," Angela responded, clearly conveying that something about her mom's words and tone sounded a little bit crass.

"You know what I mean, honey. Kenny's got his college education, he's going into a good profession—teaching—and he wants you to get your education too. He accepts me, he accepts your sister Katherine, and he'd do anything on earth for you. Do whatever you have to do to keep him." Her mom had no doubts about Kenny or about his being an excellent choice for her elder daughter.

She went a step further and, in a near-whisper, said, "You know your sister may end up needing you and Kenny to sort of help take care of her. We all hope the vocational school thing is going to work out, but you never know . . ."

Angela knew what her mom was saying because she had heard the theme before. Her mom had a lot riding on Angela and Kenny being together, being successful, and being able—if necessary at some point in the future—to help take care of Katherine financially.

"A mother's main concerns are her children. She wants them to be happy and to be secure. That's the only way a mother can be happy and secure herself."

Clearly, her mother saw Kenny as a ticket—a ticket for all three of the Capelli women—and she did not want to hear any reluctance on Angela's part to move with Kenny to Columbus and go to college at Ohio State.

CHAPTER 15

The psychology professor wanted to get to know the Capelli girl.

"Ms. Capelli, would you please stay for a moment? I have something to ask you." He felt himself fumbling and not knowing what to do with his hands as he intercepted the very serious, focused young lady headed toward the lecture hall's exit door.

"Certainly, sir. What is it?"

The old man felt sweaty and giddy—very unsure of himself. But it felt somewhat good, reminding him of how he had felt as a young college kid himself. He had to regain some control, so he stood quietly without responding until every student was gone but her. He fantasized that she was a damsel in distress, but she seemed calm, almost relaxed now that the two of them were alone.

"You have shown exceptional qualities in my classroom, Ms. Capelli, and I was wondering if you would like to be one of my assistants." He could see she liked his attention and praise.

"Well . . . well, yes. I think so, Dr. Harding. What would I do?"

"Basically, you would help me grade papers for this class and two others, maybe help me stay at least partially organized, and maybe run errands or do whatever . . ." His voice trailed off, and he watched her closely to see if she would balk or react in a puzzled way to his vague use of the vague word "whatever."

But she didn't. She actually smiled, showing her beautifully straight teeth and a hint of sparkle in her extremely dark eyes.

"I think I can handle all that," the goddess of beauty reacted, seemingly aware of what he was fantasizing.

"Okay then. You can start next week. Check with me after Monday's class."

"Great! I will," she said as she extended her right hand to shake his then touched the back of his right hand with her left palm.

"But, Ms. Capelli, you haven't asked what the job will pay—"

"I'm not worried. I know you'll do the best that you can," the professor's suddenly intense object of affection said with self-assurance.

Chapter 16

"Guess what!" Angela greeted Kenny as soon as he walked into their newly refinished condo off Lane Avenue, just west of the sprawling OSU campus.

"What, princess?" No matter how difficult the day was, Kenny always felt his problems melt away when he came home and felt Angela's enthusiasm for life and physical embrace.

"You know my psychology prof, Dr. Harding? He wants me to work for him—grading papers, running errands—and I think sort of keeping him company."

"That's great, sweetie. That's wonderful. He's probably some lonely man, smart in some ways but dumb in others. Having you work with him, hang with him, will give him a confidence boost and will put a little excitement in his life." Obviously, Kenny was very pleased, even proud that Angela had landed some kind of job helping and accompanying an older gentleman.

"But it's more than that, Kenny." Angela wanted to make a point. "I think this could really help me too. It could help me establish myself as a professor's assistant, get some insight into how the psychology department works, who the good professors are, and make some money. I want to help pay my way as much as I can."

"Well, don't worry about that, sweetheart. I'm making pretty good money teaching, and I just sold my house down in Gallipolis. I did okay on that too."

"Maybe we should celebrate our successes!" the girl of Kenny's dreams said encouragingly.

"Great! We know how to do that, don't we?" he asked as he pulled her to him.

CHAPTER 17

Two weekends later, Kenny invited Angela to go to Scioto Downs, the harness-racing track south of Columbus. He usually went by himself, which was fine with Angela, as it gave her time to study and to maintain her tight organization. She didn't consider herself excessively meticulous, but she wanted to stay organized in all her classes and assignments.

"I'll go, but I hope you don't bet a bunch of money, sweetheart," she offered in as nicely as she could.

"You should have said, 'Money, honey.' Get it? Honey rhymes with money. Plus, you know I'm usually a big winner."

"I guess you are, *honey*, but it makes me nervous. Betting a thousand dollars on this race, a thousand dollars on that race—it makes me nervous whether you win or lose. I'm just not a gambler, a risk-taker like you. I've never had that kind of money to play with."

"I'll make you a deal, princess." Kenny was starting to negotiate. "I'll only bet a hundred dollars per race plus any accumulated winnings, and I'll quit the moment I lose."

"No, you do what you want to do. It's not right for me to try to control you. You like it, you win at it, so you should bet whatever you want. It's your money, and it's not my place to put limits on you," the caring young girl asserted, and she meant it.

"That's only one more reason I love you, Angela. You want me to be happy, and you don't try to tell me what to do. If you wanted to, it would be fine, but I guess I love you more this way."

"And I do have a surprise for you, an opportunity," Kenny nervously continued.

"Oh no—what?" But Angela was afraid she knew. Kenny had been almost too happy when she had told him about working for Dr. Harding. She thought at the time that he had seen it as something of a starting point, almost like a warm-up exercise, for bigger things, bigger things that she knew she would eventually have to face.

"There's an older gentleman, Red Conway, who owns several car dealerships here and in Florida who wants to meet you. His wife is sick, he has round-the-clock nurses for her, and I think he would pay any amount of money for occasional companionship encounters with you."

CHAPTER 18

Scioto Downs was south of Columbus on Route 23 on the way to Chillicothe, Ohio's original capital. When driving back to Gallipolis, Kenny and Angela always stopped in Chillicothe for a cup of coffee or a soda before reaching Route 35, which led into Southeast Ohio, Appalachia, and the Gallipolis Point Pleasant area.

"What is Mr. Conway going to expect from me?" Angela asked Kenny as they exited Columbus Outerbelt at 23 South.

"Nothing, princess. Just niceness and attentiveness. Just be yourself . . . Why?"

"Because I'm scared, Kenny. I'm afraid he might not like me. Maybe he'll be uncomfortable with us—you said he's a lot older than we are, right?"

"Yes, but that's good." Kenny looked mildly surprised as he tried to use his most reassuring tone of voice. "Red Conway—he'll tell you to call him Red—wants to have a good time tonight and almost escape from his life, from who he is for an evening."

"What do you mean, Kenny?" Angela thought she knew but wanted to make sure she understood. She didn't want to disappoint Mr. Conway because more importantly, that, in turn, would disappoint Kenny. She felt indebted to Kenny and obligated to pay him back for all that he had done for her and her family. If she could ever pay him back fully, she hoped she would feel a sense of freedom and of independence.

"Older men, and probably older women too, want to escape from who they are, maybe for a long time but definitely for short periods of time. Even successful guys like Red Conway want to spend an evening here, an evening there, dropping their identities and having a good time."

"So it really is an escape—they can forget about their problems, even fantasize they are someone other than who they are, which seems understandable." Angela reflected somewhat rhetorically, trying to brace herself for what might be a difficult encounter for her.

"Exactly, princess. Just like you help your Einstein buddy, Dr. Harding, you can help Red Conway. You help Dr. Harding fantasize that he's a cool guy with a certain kind of magnetism every time he walks into his office and sees you there."

"But he's never tried anything. Nothing at all. He hasn't touched me, so the whole thing is working out okay. If he started coming on to me, trying to have physical contact, I swear I'd have to quit."

"Well, Harding is a completely different person from Red Conway. Harding's an egghead. He's smart, and I'm sure he has a rich fantasy life. You've told me that he's commented about being disappointed when you're not there and that he finds comfort in your lingering fragrance and that you see him undress you with his eyes." Kenny was always reassuring, always smooth, and always selling.

"But that's my point, Kenny! I feel safe with Professor Harding because I know he's not going to try anything. He may think about it, but he's afraid to try. He doesn't want to lose me."

"Princess, that's the effect you have on me, on Harding, and you will have on every man you allow to get to know you. You will always be in the driver's seat. You will always be able to set the limits and go at your own pace."

"But, Kenny, I don't know how you can say that. Not all men are alike. This guy tonight, Mr. Conway, may expect me to go to a hotel with him tonight and offer me a bunch of money to let him do whatever he wants to do." Angela was very uncomfortable, but she didn't want to back out. She wanted Kenny to be proud of her, and she knew he was trying to teach her.

"Sweetheart, princess, I know you're uncomfortable, but you're not giving me enough credit. Do you really think I would line you up, the love of my life, with some pig that is going to try to take advantage of you? Red Conway is a very decent human being. His wife is very sick but may live for a long time. In the meantime, Red wants to have some occasional fun, to go out with a beautiful, intelligent young lady, and I *know* he will never mistreat you. In some ways, he will be like Dr. Harding, but in other ways, he'll be very different. He will want to hold hands, to play kissy-face, and to definitely have you hanging on his arm when you and he go someplace as a couple. I've screened him thoroughly, and I've made it clear to him—no full sex. You can decide to let him do some petting, but you're the one in charge—not him."

"And he's okay with all that?" Angela asked, feeling better listening to Kenny explain things.

"Absolutely!" Kenny said without hesitation.

"You'll be just as safe with Red as you are with your prof. The professor wants to have strictly a mental affair with you. Red wants to have kind of a good-time affair with you, an emotional affair where he can forget about his wife's illness. As far as that goes, he's assured me that he would never cheat on his wife," Kenny said, further trying to reassure.

"But that's only half the problem, Kenny. Don't you see?" Angela asked.

"See what, princess?"

"The word *cheating* covers a wide range of activities. What's cheating to one man may not be cheating to another."

"You're right," Kenny conceded. "But what's the other half of the problem?"

"What's he going to want if and when his wife dies? At that point, nothing would really be considered cheating."

"Well, if you and he hit it off and have a long-term relationship, I guess we'll have to see . . . But remember, tonight, tomorrow, and any nights in the future—you are the person in charge. You can draw the line wherever you want," Kenny said as he reached over and held both of her hands in a firm grasp.

"And no matter what you do with any other man, I will know that I'm the one you really love and that I'm the only man you make real love with."

CHAPTER 19

Red Conway was just as Kenny had described him and even more. He was a tall, obviously wealthy gentleman whose white hair contrasted sharply with his tanned skin.

"You seem like a man who wants to have a fun evening," Angela said soon in their conversation.

Kenny had left the two of them alone—it was obvious—so that they could get comfortable. Kenny busied himself going to the bathroom, buying scouting reports, and watching other contests on the numerous TVs surrounding the private loge area.

"I really do, Angela," responded the physically fit Red, whose smoothly coiffed hair probably had been dark auburn at one time.

"Tell me about this horse racing thing," Angela queried. This was her first time watching horses race, pulling little carts with a rider in each cart.

"These are trotters, honey. Those little buggies the jockeys are in are called sulkies. You like 'em?" Red, the seemingly consummate gentleman, asked.

"I *think* I do . . . I'll let you know as the evening progresses." Angela admiringly watched as the trotters rhythmically ran warm-up laps.

"I think it's very difficult to train a horse to be a trotter. It takes a special breed or something plus training from the time they're old enough to walk steady," Red added.

"You seem to know quite a bit about them," Angela responded, trying to be nice and to keep the conversation going.

"Well, not too much, but I've owned a couple of trotters—"

"*That's* how you know so much about them. Do you still own them? I'd love to see them, you know, see them in their stables, maybe take them for a little ride in a *sulky*," Angela said with genuine excitement in her young voice.

"Well, I sold the horses after a year or two. I learned it's not a way to make money. In fact, it's a good way to lose money—fast."

"But if you enjoyed it, it was probably worth it, wasn't it?" Angela asked.

"Sure, but I lost interest in them. Like a lot of things in life, they were nice to dabble in for a while, but long term, I prefer steadier, more predictable things. You know—sure bets."

"Did your horses win some races? Did you make money betting on them?" Angela asked with more than a hint of eagerness.

"Yes and no, honey. Yes, they won a few races, but no, I never made money betting on them."

"You never bet on them for a race they won?" she asked with a that's-hard-to-believe tone.

"Oh, I won some money on a race here and there, but in the long run, I lost a hell of a lot more money than I won."

"I understand," Angela reacted, sympathetic and disappointed.

"Oh, don't feel bad, darling. I never bet any money I couldn't afford to lose. I'm not like most gamblers, probably 95 percent of the ones here tonight."

"How's that?" she asked.

"Most gamblers, if they're not actually addicted, believe that they'll get their turn eventually. They talk themselves into believing that after a series of losses, they're 'due'—due to hit the jackpot to finally make up for all the losses they've racked up."

"That's not the way probability theory works, though, is it?" Angela asked but then instantly recognized that Red's frame of reference was not theoretical or based on book learning.

"I'm sure you're right, but I don't really know what probability theory is," Red answered with no embarrassment, his penetrating blue eyes looking directly into her extremely dark almost-purple eyes. "I just know that people need to be careful not to spend a bunch of money they don't have, hoping to get rich."

"You mean get something for nothing?" Angela wanted to know. She was very quickly learning to enjoy this newfound gentleman. She liked that he was knowledgeable but listened to what she had to say and was not afraid to admit he didn't know something, like the probability theory thing.

"It's sort of about getting something for nothing, but the gamblers I've seen feel they deserve it. After all the money they've spent over the years, winning doesn't seem like something for nothing. If anything, they feel they've *earned* it. They've spent enough money as they see it that they're finally getting the payoff from their investment. They think they deserve it. But I've learned some other things too," Red said, thoroughly enjoying the conversation with this gorgeous young lady.

"What?" The lady's eyes got bigger. She was finding Red's common sense, wealth, and worldly wisdom attractive.

"First of all, most people never get the payoff, and second, if they do, they quickly blow it."

"Why do they throw away what they've won?" Angela wondered.

"I suppose different people have different ways of looking at it, but I think most of them convince themselves they're now getting 'on a roll,' and they'd better make the most of it while they can."

"But aren't some of the winners smart enough to set aside a big chunk of their winnings and just continue to gamble with what's left?"

"Not really, honey. Not the ones I've seen win big. Take Kenny, for example. He's won more money than most big-time gamblers who are twice his age. And he always pours it right back into the hands of evil Lady Luck."

"Yeah . . ." Angela's voice trailed off. She felt scared, even a little nauseous. Red Conway had put into words something she had feared but had been afraid to ask Kenny about. Kenny always seemed to have a lot of money yet always seemed to need more. For some time now, she had suspected but had not wanted to ask. She suspected Kenny had a gambling problem.

"There are people in this world who make tremendous money from gambling," Red continued. His eyes had a glint to them, and he suddenly looked more like a shrewd businessman than a fun-loving, fatherly type out for a relaxing evening.

"You mean like the owners of racetracks and casinos?" Angela asked, assuming she was correct.

"Well, yes, but people even higher up on the food chain than the owners. The people whose business it is to make sure that human nature— the urge to gamble, to win—doesn't change."

Angela sensed that Red knew a lot he wasn't telling, sort of a story behind the headlines, but she also sensed that he had said all that he wanted to say.

CHAPTER 20

The next morning, quite early, Angela and Kenny were awakened by the telephone ringing.

"Hello?" Angela said the greeting as though asking a question. She sensed, actually knew, that it was Red Conway calling.

"Good morning, Angela. It's Red. I hope I didn't wake you up." His voice sounded tentative and nervous, almost shaky.

"Well, not really. Kenny and I were just starting to think about rolling out of bed," Angela said, stretching the truth as Kenny nodded his approval in rapid short movements.

"I think I did wake you up, and I'm sorry. I just wanted to tell you what an incredible time I had last night with you, and I wanted to see if you're free for lunch today." Red sounded a little calmer, like a schoolboy who was over his initial butterflies when calling whom he thought was the prettiest girl in the class for the first time.

"I think I could be free for lunch today," Angela responded, trying to sound warm as Kenny's head continued to bob. "What do you have in mind?"

"I'm hoping you'll let me send a car to pick you up. My personal driver, Russ, will bring you to my office. I'll show you around, and then we can scoot over to Sammy's for some salad and grilled fish. Sound good?"

"Yes, I'll be ready," Angela responded, this time with a sense of anticipation that surprised her a little. She had been to Sammy's in German Village, south of Downtown Columbus, but only for dinner. Actually, she didn't know they were open for lunch.

"You're a great girl, Angela. I haven't stopped thinking about you since last night. I hardly slept at all," Red Conway spoke in a tone of true confessions. "Russ will pick you up around eleven."

"Okay, Mr. Conway, I mean Red. I'm looking forward to it," Angela said with feelings.

"Not as much as I am—believe me. Bye, baby."

Red quickly hung up as if relieved to have completed what he had been thinking about and silently rehearsing since four in the morning. Something about this girl was different, special.

He was accustomed to being in command of people surrounding him and in charge of his own feelings. Angela, without so much as saying or doing anything in particular, had turned the tables. As soon as he met her, he had felt vulnerable. Instead of being confident and forceful, he had felt unsure of himself and somewhat restrained.

He hadn't wanted to make a bad impression and apparently had not. She had laughed, eyes sparkling when he had tried to say funny things. She had looked innocent but welcoming when he had touched her hand. And she hadn't pushed his hand away when he had rested it on her thigh.

CHAPTER 21

"Ms. Capelli, I am Russ. Are you ready to go?" The driver was a light-skinned man of color who rang the doorbell at the townhouse at ten fifty.

"Well, yes. I'm ready, Russ. Would you like to step in for a moment while I grab my coat?"

"No, ma'am. I'm fine here," Russ said as he stood on the concrete stoop. Russ was big, friendly, and looked as if he could double as a bodyguard. Angela felt him looking at her with a slight squint, probably sizing her up and trying to figure out what she and Mr. Conway were going to be doing together.

He opened the passenger's rear door for Angela and extended his arm and opened palm to signal for her to get in.

"Thanks, Russ!" Angela wanted to be polite and found it easy to be that way with most people.

She and Russ laughed and made a light conversation as she alternated between easing back into the rich leather seat and leaning forward to listen to Russ. She learned that he was a retired Columbus cop, had done undercover work, and had been friends with Red Conway for years before Red finally convinced him to retire and come to work for him.

"Yeah, Mr. Conway and I go way back. We've helped each other out of some sticky situations, if you know what I mean. I'm totally loyal to him. I've got his back and would do absolutely anything that he needed me to do."

"I know what you mean," Angela said, but she didn't really want to imagine. The more she looked closely at Russ, the more she was concluding that he was a bodyguard, with scars to confirm it. She liked him but felt that in the wrong situation, he could be a thug. Something was scary about him too, in that she sensed that nothing scared him. Risking his life or a limb seemed to be a small wager for him if he were doing what he believed he was supposed to do.

People without any seeming fear of death were scary to Angela. At times Kenny acted that way, opening up his Corvette as fast as it would go on trips to and from Gallia County. Respectfully, he didn't do this when Angela was with him.

CHAPTER 22

The time went fast as Angela and Russ exceeded the speed limit all the way to Lancaster, home to Red Conway's original dealership and moderately posh office perched above the nearly glittering showroom.

Russ escorted her swiftly through the showroom, ignoring the staff of onlookers, all eager to meet and greet prospects. They could only speculate about just who this gorgeous, raven-haired young lady was. One thing they knew she wasn't, though, and that was a bimbo. The old man was clearly upgrading.

"Angela, darling, come in!" Red strode by his executive assistant Marge to embrace Angela. She hugged him warmly in return.

"Marge, this is the young psychologist, budding marketing guru I told you about. Say hi to Angela. Angela, this is Marge, who's been with me as personal secretary, personnel director, and family friend for twenty-five years. She and my wife Helen were in the same sorority at Ohio State."

"It's nice to meet you, Marge." Angela looked directly at Marge and extended her hand.

"Likewise, I'm sure," Marge responded dryly. Angela could tell immediately that Marge didn't like her and would later learn from Red that Marge didn't like any woman other than Helen or herself to look at or talk to Red.

"It's nothing personal, believe me," Red would later reassure Angela.

"Shall we take a five-minute tour and then head to lunch?" Red was all smiles and very excited.

Angela is even more striking in daylight hours than at night, if that were possible, Red thought. She had natural beauty and didn't need to apply much time or makeup in order to glow. She seemed to be very calm, very secure, especially for someone her age. *Maybe anybody who looked that good would be secure,* Red thought to himself.

Kenny must be a fool, Red thought. *How could any man, even one who burned through money the way Kenny did, let his woman go out with other men? Even though Angela seemed secure, Kenny didn't.*

If I get something going with Angela, I may have Kenny to deal with, Red reflected to himself. It sure felt good to have Russ on the payroll.

CHAPTER 23

"I have a surprise for you, sweetie!" Red exclaimed as soon as Marge left, closing the door behind her.

"What?" Angela responded excitedly.

"We're going to go back to Scioto Downs this afternoon, but you have to get dressed first."

"W-what do you mean?" Angela responded with a touch of embarrassment, worried that maybe her clothes didn't look right. At a deeper level, she wondered if Red was already trying to figure out a way to get her undressed.

"We're gonna get you into the stables, visit some horses, and then ride in a sulky around the racetrack. Something you've wanted to do ever since last night—right?"

"Oh yeah!" Angela's excitement instantly returned.

"Marge was able to find some clothes to fit you and make you look like a real honest-to-goodness jockey," Red said as he opened a closet behind his desk, revealing dark brown boots, tight-fitting pants, a blousy orange-and-white satin shirt, with a matching head gear. Attached to the helmet was a pair of amber-shaded goggles secured by dark brown straps.

"Oh my god, Red! You are unbelievable!" Angela started out loudly, but her voice faded quickly as her eyes welled up with tears.

"Quit that, baby. This is all about fun—doing what we want to do, maybe even dreamed of doing. You're beautiful. I've got some money, so we might as well enjoy it. If you get sad, it'll make me sad."

"Oh, Red. I'm not sad—I'm happy! I'm thrilled, actually, that you want to do things for me to make me happy. Like I said, you're unbelievable— you're incredible!" Angela felt Red pull her close to him, and she stood on her tiptoes to kiss him. Her eyes closed, and she tried to pretend she was kissing Kenny.

But it didn't feel the same. It wasn't the same.

Red Conway was taller, bigger, burlier, and seemed less skillful than Kenny, but not less passionate.

"Let's take a quick tour, then let Russ take us to Sammy's. From there, we'll zip down to Scioto. You can change in the jockeys' dressing rooms."

That afternoon was the beginning of a whirlwind relationship between Angela and Red.

CHAPTER 24

The relationship between Angela and Kenny did not seem to be enhanced by his encouraging her to get involved with people like Red Conway. In fact, their relationship didn't seem to be growing or deepening.

They were two very busy people, caught up in their individual lives, lives that were separate but that were bonded around activities that made Angela feel ashamed.

Angela was a full-time student, and the time and attention Dr. Harding required were expanding.

"You should be pleased that the good doctor is thriving on your care and feeding, honey," Kenny would say. "Do you think he has any money?"

Angela knew where Kenny wanted to go with this conversation, and she threw up roadblocks before he could get there. "I think he and his wife live on the money he makes. They don't have extra money to spend on entertainment. Plus, his wife watches every penny he spends. When he buys us lunch or has a pizza delivered, I can tell he's spending money he has hoarded. You know, hidden from her."

Kenny rolled his eyes upward, striking a pensive pose, and responded, "Who knows? Maybe he's been hiding money from her for years. Maybe he's got a few thou hidden somewhere."

"Kenny, I'm sure he doesn't," Angela reacted with a touch of irritation in her voice. She never liked it when Kenny used words like "thou" instead of thousand or "mill" instead of million, projecting himself as a wealthy big shot or a "high-roller" as he thought. Besides, Dr. Harding was a nice man, a somewhat pitiful man, whose constant fawning and watching her every move was quite a bit for her to bear.

She knew Kenny would like for her to get more seductive with Dr. Harding, allow him to pet her, for example, if there was any chance at all that the professor could start paying two or three hundred a week for the excitement.

"Please, Kenny, don't encourage me to do something I really, really don't want to do. It just wouldn't be comfortable or in any way right to get Dr. Harding further turned on or aroused about me. He's fine with where the relationship is right now. I know he likes his fantasy life about me and him, but I know he would be scared to death to act on it—"

"Okay, okay," Kenny interrupted.

"Let me finish, please. He's getting from this relationship all that he wants, all that he can handle. And for me, it creeps me out just thinking about doing anything more with him. He's not my type, and he seems like an old man and one I feel sorry for too," she concluded.

Kenny wouldn't quite drop it. "He's not as old as Red Conway."

"That's different, and you know it. Red's a lot younger acting, he's fun, and he wants to take me places and show me off."

"All right, all right." Kenny was ready to drop it. But Angela knew he was starting to be bothered by all the time and attention Red was dedicating to her. The money he gave her, the "financial support" as he called it, was incredible. Kenny liked the income, but Angela knew he was developing jealousy toward Red and maybe toward the relationship she and Red enjoyed.

CHAPTER 25

"I need to talk with you," Red said hurriedly and somewhat hoarsely on the phone to Angela one Friday morning.

"What's wrong? Is everything okay?" Angela detected worry in Red's voice, and she suspected he had further bad news regarding his wife. She had not been doing well of late, particularly for the last six months that Red and Angela had been seeing each other during Red's every free moment.

They had gone to dinner innumerable times, New York City twice, and Naples, Florida, five times. Red loved his home in Naples, perched on a small peninsula that jutted into the gulf.

It had been during their first visit to Naples that Red had very much wanted to have complete intimacy with Angela, and she had obliged.

"How do you feel, sweetie?" Red asked after what had been, for Angela, a brief but satisfying lovemaking encounter, nothing extraordinary but nice.

"I feel good, I guess, but I feel strange," she answered honestly. Before he could ask her to explain "strange," she continued, "I've never made love with anyone but Kenny, and I guess for a long time, I never thought I would. I love Kenny, and he's always said I could have sex with other men, but I could only make love with him."

"What we just did, for me, was not just sex. It was the real thing. It was love," the usually certain-of-himself Red said with passion that had not cooled down.

"It was! It was! I felt love too, Red, but now that it's over, it seems like I have a lot to think about. You know, trying to figure out how I feel and why I feel that way."

"Well, don't let this mess up our relationship," Red reacted, but he didn't really think it would.

"How so?" Angela wondered out loud.

"Sometimes making love complicates a relationship. You know what they say in the magazines and advice columns? 'Going to bed with someone is a notch on the bed for the man and an act of intimacy for the woman.'"

"My psych professor says that, but I don't know if that's true anymore," Angela murmured, admiring his nearly nude, athletic physique as they both lay propped up in the massive bed, facing toward the water and setting sun.

"Well, it's not true for us. I can tell you that. You and I have a kind of pure relationship. It has been clear from the start that we like each other and get along well. I want to spend time with you, Angie, and you can use some financial support. There are really no strings attached."

"What do you mean 'no strings attached'?" Angela didn't like the idea that this was, more or less, a business relationship. What she had with Dr. Harding felt like a business relationship, and that was okay. But if she and Red just had some kind of barter arrangement, that didn't feel so good. She wanted to feel that in some way, at some level, he loved her and she loved him.

"I just feel that we made love because we both *wanted to*." Red continued, "We didn't, or rather you didn't feel obligated to make love, did you?"

"No, I really didn't. I was hoping we would, eventually, and this afternoon was a perfect time. You were wonderful. You were beautiful, and we were good together, don't you think?"

"I really do," the big man said as he smiled comfortably. "Who knows, maybe we'll both want to do it again sometime. Sometime soon, I hope."

"I hope so too," she said as she pulled herself to him, kissed him, and discovered he was ready to make love again.

CHAPTER 26

As the weeks went on, the "strange" feeling did not go away for Angela. She liked Red; she enjoyed being with him. He was a powerful man she admired, but after making love, she always felt a little bit down or depressed. She felt nervous or "on edge." She found herself subtly trying to sidestep opportunities for making love with him.

The hoarseness in Red's voice on the phone on this Friday morning was unusual. He never seemed to get tense or worried.

"Is your wife okay?" Angela had asked.

"Yes, she's okay. Okay for her, which is one day at a time. Just let Russ pick you up—he's on his way now, and we can talk when you get here."

"Where?" she asked, not certain where Red was.

"I'll be at home, waiting for you. I'll see you soon—love you." And with that, Red hung up the phone.

Angela tried to be friendly and upbeat with Russ as he raced the limo toward Red's home. But Russ was very good at "reading" people, including their body language and other nuances.

"You don't seem yourself, Angel. What's wrong?" he finally asked. Somehow, Angela liked it that Russ called her Angel. He was the only person who had ever done that, but she imagined that her father might call her that if he were alive.

"I don't know. I just feel kind of scared." Angela had determined weeks ago that she could trust Russ and that she could be honest with him. Besides, what was the worst that could happen? He might tell Red, his boss, but it wouldn't matter. Angela would tell Red almost anything also.

"What are you scared about, Angel? You can tell Uncle Russ." Russ really liked the beautiful girl with the knockout eyes and body. He even admired her in many ways and fought to keep from indulging in sexual fantasies when he was with her.

"Red sounded worried, concerned. You know, not his usual upbeat self. I asked him if it was about his wife, but he said no."

"Well, I don't have a clue about what's bothering him. I really don't," Russ responded without hesitation. Angela knew he was telling the truth, but she wasn't fishing for information anyway.

"The good news is," Russ continued, "I'm sure he will tell you when you see him. Red, like all of us, totally believes in you and trusts you." Both Russ and Angela knew the phrase "like all of us" basically meant Russ himself.

The gates to Red's estate opened as the limo approached, and Russ continued to drive with some degree of urgency. Red must have told him to pick up Angela and deliver her ASAP but without an explanation why.

The mature trees lining the gentle uphill driveway seemed to be speeding the opposite direction as the limo scurried almost silently.

Very unlike himself, Red was standing on the pillared front porch, probably having been pacing, as Russ delivered his exciting but worried package.

CHAPTER 27

"Talk to me, Red . . ." Angela needed to know what was upsetting him and, in turn, upsetting her. It didn't feel right that she could have gotten so upset, nearly panicky, triggered by Red's tone of voice on the phone a short time earlier.

"I want to. I'm going to, sweetie. I will only be truthful. I thought about how best to tell you, but there is no good way. Please, let's sit down."

They sat on the tufted large beige sectional in Rod's huge family room, and Angela began to see Red Conway the businessman appear. Red Conway, a good man, a basically honest man, but not a man to try to take advantage of.

He had not achieved his success in the new and used car sales business by being a pushover. He wasn't especially shrewd, but he always trusted his instincts. And if someone tried to manipulate him in a way he didn't want to be manipulated, he recoiled. He drew back and poised for a strike, calculating the time that would be best for him.

"Your boyfriend Kenny is in over his head, Angela," Red said with a harshness, with a glare that Angela immediately found offensive.

"What's that supposed to mean?" she asked with a tone of defensiveness that they both noticed.

"I know you're not going to like this, and I don't say that I blame you. I just want you to hear me out—let me tell you what I know, what I'm absolutely sure of, and then we can speculate about anything else that is going on. Okay?"

Angela nodded and was surprised to realize she was crying.

Red, the strong businessman, plowed forward. "Kenny makes a lot of money, wins a lot of money, but he always needs more. You don't have to agree or disagree. I knew him before I knew you, and he was always a guy who dropped a load at the track and worked real hard to convince everybody that it didn't really bother him. But you know me, and you know my hobby of studying gamblers. I knew it bothered him and that he was cultivating the belief that the big score was just around the corner. So he kept right on betting, pouring more and more money down the rat hole."

"I hear you, Red. I do. So what does this mean? What is the problem right now?" Angela felt she had to push Red to tell her immediately what was going on.

"Kenny's in debt. Big debt. He's leveraged everything and has no real way to pay it back. I'm sorry, sweetie, but he's in trouble."

"How bad is the trouble?" Angela asked as she felt her abdomen collapsing from inside. She suddenly recognized she was part of Kenny's leveraging everything he could for money.

"He's at least $300,000 in debt, which, I know, is hard to believe."

"I just find it incredulous. I really do." She wanted to run, to wake up—to do something that would erase the pain and fear. The jeopardy. If Kenny was in trouble, so was she.

She owed a lot to Kenny. Had it not been for him, she might still be stuck in Gallipolis, a "river rat," listening to someone extol the virtues and beauties of living on or near the Ohio River.

"I've seen it. Now I'm ready to move on." She remembered Kenny having said about the Ohio River when he first told her he wanted to get a job in Columbus.

"Red, I want to do something. I want to help Kenny get out of this jam. I owe it to him. You must be able to come up with an idea, a plan. Can't you help him? Can't you help me?" She reached over and hugged the burly man who seemed to hug her back without feeling.

Angela frowned and was inwardly angry because it appeared that Red had already figured out a solution and was extremely matter-of-fact as he began to tell her what it was. She didn't like the way he unconsciously avoided eye contact and spoke rapidly as he laid out what needed to be done.

It was as if he took several steps back emotionally, detached himself from the situation and from her. She saw the coldness, the self-absorption of Red Conway the businessman. He was no longer Red Conway the boyfriend or man friend or even sugar daddy. He was no longer the soft, gentle, and "let me take care of your every need" lover.

He was a man who had gotten involved with a much younger woman, initially having been solicited by her live-in boyfriend. He had spent quite a bit of money but had enjoyed every minute of it.

Now, though, it was time to cut his losses. To Red's way of thinking, this crudely charismatic Corvette speedster was trouble. He was in over his head, and probably this girlfriend was going to end up in a bad way too.

Now that Red was sensing the gravity of the situation—maybe even life threatening for Kenny—he wanted to get the hell out of the situation. Again, it had been fun, but with the risks, it was no longer worth it. He was thinking of his own reputation, his own skin.

Now that he himself was this close to danger, this closely affiliated with someone who might end up in a morgue someplace, he had started losing sleep and losing the ability to concentrate.

For weeks, he hadn't been troubled in the least with the emotion that now stalked him night and day. It wasn't until his own make-believe existence and personal safety were threatened that he suddenly suffered unrelentingly. The torment came from within himself—the emotion was guilt.

CHAPTER 28

"Kenny borrowed money he can't repay from a German-based syndicate. I don't know much about it, but I know this syndicate has infiltrated much of the off-track betting in this country." Red seemed weary and seemed to know some things he was choosing not to tell.

"I don't understand," Angela responded. For a split second, Red started to feel sorry for her as she began to tremble and cry again. Then he caught himself, refocused, and pushed ahead.

"This syndicate is basically a pooling of money by a few super rich German businessmen who remain anonymous, out of harm's way, and reap the benefits of exorbitant interest rates. They find people like Kenny at racetracks, casinos, and offer to back them financially."

"You mean like loan sharks?"

"Sort of . . . but these guys are in a whole 'nother league. They have billions of collateral, they never get dirty, and they seem to be able to operate outside the purview of the Feds. They see their business as a no-lose proposition. They find someone like Kenny, get him on the hook, and good things happen. If he happens to get out of his downward spiral and start winning again, he pays them back. And they've had a short-term lending rate that anybody would love."

"But you told me before, Red, gamblers really don't win. They just delay the inevitable," Angela said through somewhat clenched teeth.

"Yeah, that's what I believe, but supposedly, this group has actually funded some big-time gamblers, like Hollywood types, who have stayed in Lady Luck's arms for a long time. I'm sure that's what they prefer—finding a gambler who really makes money for a long, long time. With this kind of gambler, they can be the financial backers."

"So they bet on the gamblers?" she asked, feeling like she was beginning to understand but not finding any comfort in doing so.

"Yep. That's right."

"But what about Kenny?" she asked, clearly worried.

"I think they've given up on him. He looked good at first, actually for a while, but petered out. Like a jack after you draw two kings, they're ready to discard him."

"Jesus, Red, we've gotta tell him."

"No, I don't think so," the gentleman whom Angela used to think was so wise said. "In fact, I feel sure he doesn't want you to know the trouble he's in. You're his princess, his angel on a pedestal. He—"

"Well, what are we going to do?" she interrupted. "I know you have a plan—I can tell by looking at you. What is it?"

Red hung his head as he began, "I have reason to believe one of the investors in the syndicate is Wolfgang Werner. He's a fellow who comes from generations of money and who, on the surface, is squeaky-clean. He retired early from U.S. Steel in Pittsburgh.

"He has a son, Fredrik, whom he's worried about. The old man is a total conservative, a traditionalist with black-and-white views on everything. In a nutshell, he thinks Junior might be gay or at least undecided. Apparently, the boy has gone out a few times with girls, but his dad ventured down to Athens, Ohio, once and jumped to the conclusion that at least two or three of the boy's fraternity brothers were gay."

Angela was now feeling sick, queasy, and trapped. She knew where Red was headed.

"I told Wolfgang I might be able to help him, I mean help his son. I put two and two together and thought I could help Fredrik and his dad."

"So you want me to go down to Athens and fuck Junior?" Angela shocked Red and herself a bit with her crudeness. Too much was happening all at once. And she felt certain that Red knew more about all this than he was telling. How did he "have reason to believe" that this Wolfgang was part of this German outfit? How did he, Red, even know this man?

Angela was learning suddenly, though was not totally surprised, that her longtime boyfriend and committed partner was over his head in gambling debts and that the foreign loan sharks might "collect" the old-fashioned way.

She also was coming face-to-face with the fact that Red was first and foremost out for himself. He was a businessman, a self-made, self-centered car dealer who was sending vibes that he was ready to "break up." Maybe he needed to confess to his sick wife and get her forgiveness before she died.

Angela was also discovering that she had been cajoled and seduced into a way of life, a kind of double or triple existence that was self-destructive. *"I'm so busy taking care of men—Kenny, Red, Professor Harding—that I don't have time for me. I need to get the hell out of this situation. I need to carve out or build a life for me and learn to make myself a priority—a priority to me!"*

She wanted to scream this out to Red right now and to Kenny and the professor later, but instead, she thought these thoughts silently but forcefully to herself.

But she knew she would need to try to fix things first. She would feel obligated to go to Athens, do what she could to help this Fredrik "go hetero" in order to get Kenny off the hook. Probably, the dad was willing to throw in a hundred thousand or so to help his son, and Red would make up the difference. That way, both men could feel they had done something good and humane. They could both feel like good people, taking care of others—the German guy could feel he was saving his son from a life of misery, and Red could feel he was perhaps saving Kenny's life.

Neither of them was giving thought to her, the pawn in this high-priced therapy. Maybe Red was because he was trying to help her buy Kenny's way out of his jeopardy. At the same time, maybe Red was trying to make the final payment on his six months of fun—no, exhilaration.

"Oh, God, if you just let me get through this, let me fix things for Kenny to save his life, I swear I'll never get involved in this kind of craziness again. I don't want to be used or to be a user. I just want to have a normal life. Please, God. Please!"

It was starting to seem clear that once she got Kenny free and clear of the syndicate, she would need to leave him. She would have repaid him; she would have given him what he had given her—a decent shot at a better life.

She loved Kenny, but she felt that love eroding. The things she had admired about him when she first dated him were now not so important or seemed rather superficial. She was finding it increasingly hard to respect her first love.

CHAPTER 29

Gallipolis seemed like a long way away as Angela drove down Route 33 from Columbus through Lancaster on her way to Athens. She remembered starting to work at the clothing store where her grandfather had worked. She had just turned fourteen and had started to make money to support the family. The wages were barely minimum, but they helped out a lot.

She had found herself suddenly thrust into a role as breadwinner. Young and naïve, she hadn't recognized what that meant in terms of responsibility. She had felt some of the insecurity and depression that might accompany the role of taking on the burden of caring for a parent. She had grown up fast in some ways, but her maturing had lagged behind in other ways.

Fairly quickly, she had become dependent on Kenny. Accepting the money he freely doled out to her was at first embarrassing but gradually came to be reinforcing, even encouraging. Angela began to see that just by being nice, by being attentive, she and her family could live fairly well. It made her feel somewhat secure as well as positive about her worthiness to have plenty of money to help support her family and enough left over to buy whatever she wanted.

As she drove by the sprawling Conway dealership in Lancaster, her mind jumped to Red. Somehow, she had morphed from being exclusively Kenny's woman to being almost available for hire by a rich man like Red.

Red was a decent man, probably had a lot of issues she didn't know about yet had always treated her like a lady. He had never yelled at her, criticized her, or belittled her. He had always been gentle and respectful.

Now that I know quite a bit about psychology, I'm learning that my life is really fucked up, she thought to herself.

For years, I've felt pretty good about myself and have grown in confidence. I guess my self-esteem has increased, but it's been based a lot on my relationship with Kenny and now Red, and both relationships are screwed up. Both men use me for themselves, and I use them too. Both men get their male egos pumped by me, and I get this sense of power, appeal, and competence from being with them and getting money.

It's too much like my friend Sally warned me it would be—'selling out' on my values in order to live whatever my young girl's fantasy was about the 'good life.' My life on the surface is good, but down deep, I'm not taking good care of me. I'm taking care of a couple of men, enjoying what the money does, but it's wrong. Maybe I shouldn't blame myself and say my life has been wrong, but rather, what I'm doing today is no longer right for me.

My boyfriend, a Svengali who came along when I was desperate to latch onto a means of improving my life, is in very serious, maybe life-or-death trouble. Because of his problem with gambling, he set me up to entertain a rich car dealer. Now the car dealer has set me up to entertain or do some kind of weird therapy with a college student—to help him discover the benefits of sex with a woman as opposed to sex with a man.

Oh, God, please help me get out of this mess. I know I have done this to myself, and I beg for forgiveness. If I can just accomplish this mission in Athens at Ohio University, I swear I will straighten up and never sin again. I need strength and your forgiveness—forgiveness for what I've done and forgiveness for what I have to do in Athens.

CHAPTER 30

The Sigma Chi house on Park Place in Athens sat impressively back from the street, with a large front yard that was worn from too many touch football games and general roughhousing. The outside lights were needlessly turned on, and the deejay on the front porch was playing pop music at an inviting volume. He would crank it up louder as the evening wore on and the sobriety dissipated.

"It's nice to meet you, Fredrik," Angela found herself saying to the awkwardly built fellow with a crew cut who was off to the side at the Sigma Chi monthly open house.

She had sought him out, recognizing him from a picture Red had given her.

Somehow, it seemed self-protective and an important part of her plan to use a different name. "Hi, I'm Marie." Angela had giggled, knowing how to captivate a self-conscious guy like Fredrik almost instantly.

"Marie, Marie, where have you been all my life?" the young man from Sigma Chi asked, trying to act poised and confident. It was clear that beneath his façade was a guy who wasn't what he wanted to be.

"Just trying to grow up and meet interesting people," Angela Marie responded.

"What do you mean?" Fredrik asked, somewhat puzzled.

"Well, you asked where I've been all your life, and I was just trying to tell you that I've been in the process of growing up and meeting lots of people along the way. But I must say, really, that it's nice to meet you, Fredrik. It's nice to meet you here tonight," she said with a hint of a longing gaze.

Her warm large eyes melted Fredrik. He did not want to telegraph it, but no girl, no woman, and especially one who was drop-dead gorgeous had ever been this responsive to him. Not even close.

Fredrik was captivated and astonished. He was astounded that this girl from Ohio State just happened to be in Athens, Ohio, to meet up with one of her girlfriends and drop by the Sigma Chi open house. Fortunately for him, he surmised, the girlfriend had gotten sick and never showed up.

Marie ended up alone at the fraternity house and, as incredible as it seemed, showed more than a friendly interest in Fredrik. "Whatever I'm wearing, whatever I'm doing, I've got to remember," he said aloud.

"What?" Marie reacted, grabbing his arm and pulling him closer to make sure she understood. He seemed to fascinate her as she was totally attentive to him.

"I just mean that you're the most beautiful girl in the world, and you came over and introduced yourself to me. I don't know what it is about me that attracted any attention from you, whatsoever."

"I warn you, Fredrik, I'm a psych major, and I try to 'read between the lines' and interpret everything people say."

"Okay, what am I saying, or what am I really saying?" It was going to be hard for him to sound intelligent or feel intelligent because he was so preoccupied with her beauty and with the fact that she was so interested in his words and his every little nuance. He found himself feeling overwhelmed and wanting the evening to last forever.

CHAPTER 31

"Where are you staying while you're here?" Fredrik asked as the partygoers began to thin out, some pairing off to wander over to the university's golf course. With bottles and blankets underneath their arms, their intentions were to drink and make out.

A double entendre was commonly used to compare sexual activities with golfing. One of Fredrik's fraternity brothers even announced loudly as he and "Boney Joanie," a notorious one-night stand left the party early, "I'm going to play a little night golf—hopefully, I'll get a hole in one!"

Joanie, thin as a rail, smiled knowingly with surprisingly plump lips. She clung to her date for the evening and even felt for his genitals casually.

"I guess I'll stay wherever you want me to stay," Angela cooed seductively, well aware that Fredrik was readily seducible by her. *Maybe he's not really gay after all*, she thought to herself. He seemed sort of effeminate but, mostly, somewhat shy and self-conscious.

Maybe he never had a strong male role model, she continued thinking. Maybe women had raised him, or maybe, just maybe, he was actually bisexual. She was confident she would find out the answers to these and other speculations within the subsequent twenty-four-hour period.

"How about if I get you a room at the University Inn? It's not far from here, and I have a car."

"That sounds good, big boy." He had already told her he wasn't called Fred, Freddie, or any other nicknames. "Why don't we just go in my car though?" she continued. "I need someplace to park it overnight, and this way, it will be safe."

"Okay, the inn is not that far—I can jog back."

"Don't be silly, Fredrik. And don't disappoint me. I want you to spend the night with me. Grab a change of clothes for tomorrow, and we can go have our own party." Angela could tell Fredrik was shocked and in a serious state of disbelief. He wasn't shell-shocked, though, as he moved swiftly to comply. He returned from upstairs in two minutes with a small gym bag.

CHAPTER 32

The University Inn was south of the main campus, past the red brick dormitories of the West Green. Inside, the room was spacious, nicely refurbished, with the centerpiece being a very tall and thick king-size bed.

"Wow!" Angela said. "Look at that monster. I hope we don't get lost in there tonight."

"I'll stay close to you, Marie. I'll protect you from getting scared," Fredrik ventured out of his comfort zone to try to flirt a little and to reassure.

"Thank you, darling. I'd never be scared with you," she responded. She kissed him gently, open-mouthed, and sensed that he was tense. Oh god, she hoped it was not because he was gay and didn't even like women. She knew she was attractive and could be extremely seductive and alluring when she wanted to be. She knew she could even fake her emotions and act sexually aroused even if she was not. Sometimes, with Red and even with Kenny, she pretended to have orgasms, sometimes even big ones.

She felt Fredrik's penis firm against her pelvis. She knew he wasn't completely gay.

Gently, she helped him take off his clothes and deftly took off her own as well. She had turned off the lights in the room, and they were kissing passionately as he helped lift her into the high bed. A small beam of light was coming from the parking lot through the drapes to illuminate the room as their eyes adapted.

"Now this I like," she said as she touched Fredrik's penis and then began to rub it. His penis was not long but was wide. And it was rock hard. She knew that it was going to get the workout of its relatively inexperienced young life.

CHAPTER 33

Throughout the long night, well into the early morning of the next day, Kenny's talks about the difference between having sex and making love echoed within Angela.

The squat German boy, Fredrik, worked hard and showed tremendous stamina in order to have as much sex as he possibly could.

Angela hadn't anticipated some kind of sexual marathon. Fredrik turned out to be animal-like, unskilled in lovemaking, but determined to keep going and going and to make every moment count as long as he could.

He was not rough but not gentle either. He seemed interested in her but, at the same time, consumed with his own needs. And his needs seemed less about pleasure and more about endurance. After each ejaculation, he busied himself in an urgent kind of way, doing all that he could to achieve another erection so that they could go another round.

"Oh, Marie, I've never done this before," Fredrik said after the fourth time. He flung himself backward onto the dry side of the bed, arms extended, head rolled back, and his member shrunken.

"Oh, you're full of it—I can tell you're not even close to being a virgin," Angela, known as Marie, said.

"No, I don't mean that. I just mean I've never done it more than once on the same night."

Finally, early morning came, and Fredrik and company were exhausted. Spent.

Angela soaked in the tub, sore in some spots, but felt she had done her duty and had completed a difficult job. She had faked her feelings from beginnings to climaxes. She had tried to fantasize that she was making love with Kenny or with a celebrity, but that hadn't helped. The only thing that had helped was pretending she was in a physical workout, like an aerobics class.

Now she needed to figure out how to break off the relationship with Fredrik and how to convince Red that if Fredrik had been gay or leaning toward it, she had totally changed his orientation.

CHAPTER 34

"What time is it?" Fredrik looked terrible as Angela gazed up from the psychology textbook she was reading at the window. He rolled over and sat up in bed, modestly and gingerly pulling a sheet over his lower half.

"It's eleven o'clock, big fellow," Angela said. "How are you feeling?" she asked with a heart-melting smile.

The textbook was for her class in abnormal psychology, and she had been reading about sexual identification issues, homosexuality, and anything else that seemed pertinent. Dr. Harding could probably tell her a lot about why some people became homosexuals and lesbians and some did not. But she didn't dare ask him any questions about sexual orientation because he might misinterpret her questioning and start fantasizing more about the two of them together.

"I'm feeling like I screwed my brains out," Fredrik said with some embarrassment. "And my dick is really sore."

Angela tried to act relaxed but began to worry that Fredrik might want to have sex again.

Lunch was good; conversation was light and noncommittal. Angela skillfully asked questions, getting Fredrik to talk about himself, his family, how he ended up at Ohio University, and what he hoped to do in the future.

"My dad retired early from the steel business in Pittsburgh. He was a metallurgist—you know, studied metals and such, but eventually started a business with my grandfather. They buy and sell metals and other commodities. He wants me to come into their business right away, and I might. I'd like to start my own business first though. That's why I'm taking as many business courses, along with engineering here. I ended up at OU because my mom wanted me to go someplace close to home. Actually, she wanted me to go to college in Pittsburgh. I might have done that if I could have gotten into Carnegie-Mellon, but I couldn't. OU was close enough to home, but not too close. Now I'm sorry I didn't try to go to Ohio State though. I could have been close to you," he said as he looked away, hoping not to embarrass himself.

"Well, maybe. But to tell the truth, I've never even been to the Sigma Chi house at Ohio State. With the number of students and the size of the campus, we probably never would have met. Besides, I don't get out much. I live off campus, and I work all the time," Angela said.

"You must have lots of boyfriends in Columbus anyway." Fredrik was hoping she would say "not really."

"I have a boyfriend, but I don't know how much longer it's going to last," she said.

But Fredrik did not get his hopes up. Beautiful women like Angela always ended up with beautiful guys in the movies and in real life. But he very much wanted to believe he had been important in her life, at least for one night. He was very proud as he reminded himself he had come six times with her, and he knew the pain he was now feeling was worth it.

After seeing the highlights of the campus, including the student center, the psychology building, and the Sigma Chi house one more time, they sat on the wall near the Alpha Delta Pi house, where Angela's car was parked. Fredrik had filled her tank with gas, and she was ready to head back to Columbus.

"Fredrik, I really enjoyed all the sex last night. I think it will take me a couple of weeks to recover though."

"Me too, Marie. All my fantasies came true last night. They really did. Thank you." Fredrik kissed her with more genuine consideration and sensitivity than he had shown since they met.

"Have you ever thought you might be gay?" Angela had planned the question and had planned to ask it in just this way—seemingly as a sudden thought or query blurted out without warning.

"No, not really," Fredrik answered without hesitation. "Why do you ask?"

"Ever since you said last night you'd never done this before, I kept thinking maybe he means not with a woman—maybe he's gay! I just haven't been able to completely get it out of my mind," Angela answered dramatically.

"That's funny," Fredrik said, lightly laughing. "Was that a turn-off?"

"No, not really. In fact, it was kind of a turn-on. After that, I kept imagining I was like your sex slave, hired to turn you around, to change you from a homo to a straight." Angela watched his reaction and saw nothing negative as she used the word *homo*.

"I think my dad, maybe my mom too, worry about me being gay because I almost never bring any girl home for them to meet."

"Why not?" Angela asked.

"Two reasons, actually. One, they are both so critical. They'd pick holes in any girl I brought home. And two, I've never had the nerve to ask a good-looking girl with any class out on a date. I guess it's fear of rejection or something—you're the psychologist."

"I hope I helped you overcome any fear like that," she said as she squeezed against him.

"Believe it or not, you have," Fredrik answered with a hint of confidence.

"I don't want to keep prying, but what kind of girls have you gone out with?" Angela asked gingerly.

"Girls I paid for. You know, hookers."

CHAPTER 35

The drive to Columbus seemed long and boring. The little towns that popped up along the way were insignificant as Angela reflected on her past twenty-four hours. Her thoughts seemed random, and she didn't feel as if she could connect them all. She was feeling guilty, ashamed, and used.

She had spent the night having mechanical sex over and over with a fairly mechanical guy and was now squirming in her seat in discomfort. The guy came from a family that had lots and lots of money, but so what? If a person didn't like whom she was with, if she couldn't relate comfortably without pretending and faking, even tons of money couldn't ensure happiness.

But some money and the security it could provide were necessary. Her mom had always emphasized the importance of having enough money to get by without struggling.

The two men in her life, Kenny and Red, both had quite a bit of money, but it didn't seem to make either of them happy. Kenny gambled with his money, so he was never secure and, in fact, now had serious money problems. Red used his money to buy things, to have good times, but Angela was convinced that he was not really happy either. Beneath his kindness and generosity, Red Conway was concerned mainly about only one thing—himself.

To her way of thinking, Angela believed Red was conveniently combining several factors for his own benefit. He wanted to maintain the image of a loyal husband and stay married to his ailing wife. It did not matter that he had fairly frequent affairs with young girls, mostly good-looking girls with good bodies but not very smart. Angela knew she had been different and that Red had been developing serious feelings for her—feelings that upset his lifestyle and equilibrium. He wanted women to feel close to him, but he only wanted to pretend to feel close to them.

At this same time, Kenny was very much over his head in serious financial trouble. Red could do something pretty grandiose, even for a successful car dealer. He could negotiate a deal with a mysterious syndicate, save Kenny from purgatory on earth, or maybe something worse. At the same time, Red could try to help a young college boy go straight and break away from a young woman with whom he felt he might be falling in love.

And he could do it all without taking any risk of hurting himself.

As she drove by the Conway dealership in Lancaster, Angela knew the dating relationship with Red Conway was over. That was probably good. She gave some thought to how she could break up in a way that allowed her to preserve some sort of friendship with Red. He was a good man to have in one's corner. Maybe pulling back from Red would not be that difficult. She knew he didn't really want to be in love, so he probably would welcome some distancing in their relationship, at least temporarily.

The problem would be when he decided he wanted to escape again, perhaps take a trip together, and have sex. She convinced herself she could "turn him down without putting him down."

As for Fredrik, she hoped he would be all right. She sort of liked him in the sense that she thought he was a decent person but in no way her type. She found it ironic that he had always paid for sex prior to last night, and although he hadn't paid for it last night, someone else had done so without his knowing it.

She wanted to believe that she had helped Fredrik, that she had been something of a surrogate sex partner serving in a therapeutic capacity. She wished she had thought of that last night. She wanted to believe that as a result of their intense night together, he was now going to be able to ask nice girls out on dates and find someone who would love him and maybe help him feel better about himself. She hoped she would never know. It would definitely be better that way, to never see him again.

Kenny. Kenny was a big question mark. He was a father figure, a big brother, a lover, and a life companion. Life with him was increasingly complicated, but life without him was unimaginable.

She had felt certain when leaving Columbus yesterday that she needed to break up with Kenny. Now just twenty-four hours later, she was wondering if she should change her mind. Clearly, he had a problem, a huge problem, which she was not equipped to fix.

She may have fixed his gambling debt temporarily, but the problem was about a gambling addiction, not just a gambling debt. Dr. Harding had told her, "Show me an addict, and I'll show you a liar. Also, show me an addict, and I'll find an enabler close by who's making excuses."

She felt she had helped Fredrik with a pretty big problem—confidence and self-esteem. Maybe she could help Kenny also. Maybe his problem had to do with being in control or fearing he might lose control.

Somehow, she vowed she was going to try to change Kenny. If she could help him break his addiction, their relationship could become normal. She knew one thing—she had to break out of this whole setup of being used.

She didn't want to have sex and get paid for it. No matter what the purpose, she knew she would end up with self-disgust. She only wanted to have sex because she loved the person she was with.

Maybe it was worth a try to see if she could help Kenny. She thought she could talk Kenny into trying to get help. She probably would not tell him that, hopefully, she had settled at least part of his huge gambling debt.

Maybe she and Kenny could get some help together. It had taken two of them to get this far offtrack, and maybe some professional help—therapy or couples' counseling—could help. She was studying to be a psychologist to help people. If she believed in the profession and its capacity to help people, she and Kenny could find someone to talk to and try to work on their problems. Surely, Kenny would be open-minded to the idea or at least willing to give it a try.

Angela began to feel good about the idea of rebuilding their relationship. She and Kenny had made some mistakes, but they could change. Angela knew she could change and began to alleviate some of her guilt and shame by telling herself over and over that she would never again have sex without love.

She started thinking that she and Kenny could come through this thing better than ever, a stronger couple without all the hang-ups. Maybe it was hoping for too much, but she began fantasizing about someday getting married to Kenny, having children, and really being happy.

She made up her mind to talk with Kenny tonight and tell him almost everything. If he was asleep, she would wake him up. She would tell him about Red, the syndicate, and her mission to Athens. She might try to talk with him about his gambling problem and very much hoped he would not want to make love after they talked.

Kenny had known about her going to Athens to spend time with some rich kid Red had lined up, but he hadn't known the details.

She would fill Kenny in on some of the details that had to do with him but would definitely not tell him about the number of times she and Fredrik had had sex.

CHAPTER 36

All the air left Angela's lungs and seemed to go into her stomach and abdomen as she rounded the drive into hers and Kenny's condominium complex.

Two sheriff's cars, strobe lights piercing the dark, were parked at abrupt angles outside her front door. The lights inside the condo were not on.

Angela knew. She knew just as the little girl had known when the man from the riverboat company and the chief of police had come to their front door back in Gallipolis.

She suddenly felt like the six-year-old girl she had been and smashed on her brakes. She lost the ability to drive. She threw the lever into "park," somehow opened the door, and tumbled onto the asphalt parking lot.

She wailed; she tried to scream but couldn't. The deputies picked her up very gently and called for an emergency-rescue squad. One of the deputies, very young himself, began to cry. He had never seen a girl this beautiful. And she was distraught beyond his abilities to console.

She must already know that her live-in boyfriend had been in a one-car, high-speed crash between Jackson and Chillicothe on his way back from Gallipolis. She must already know that Kenny Chessin was dead.

PART III

CHAPTER 37

Back when the just sixteen-year-old beautiful Angela went out with the local assistant store manager in his heavily waxed and polished convertible, a twenty-year-old college student one hundred-plus miles northwest of Gallipolis was applying for an assistant store manager's position at the Victory Circle, a favorite beer and pizza spot on High Street in Columbus. Right across from the Ohio State University's inspiring gateway to advanced education, the Victory Circle was a twenty-five-year-old icon for Buckeye students and fans, especially after the scarlet and gray came out on top in their high-intensity competition.

Austin Morris grew up in Medina, Ohio, where his parents had a dairy farm and raised a few beef cattle. His dad was known throughout Medina County as a fine, upstanding man who dabbled in politics and participated seriously as a school board member. "Your father's always had a mission to help people," his devoted wife would say. "I would love to see him run for state representative, but with all the chores here at the farm, I don't see how he could spend the time he needed to spend down in Columbus at the statehouse."

Austin always suspected his dad had some secrets in Columbus that he didn't want to have overexposed.

Austin Morris left the farm and entered Ohio State, where he continued his die-hard dedication to the Buckeyes. "I'll get things all checked out for you, maybe join a fraternity, and then you can join me at OSU," he had frequently told his younger brother Nate.

"I'll sure try, but you know me and academics," Nate had frequently responded. Austin didn't think Nate had a serious problem with academics; he just never studied or seemed motivated. But he was smart in so many ways, especially socially. Nate was never at a loss for words and never seemed puzzled by the behaviors of others.

"You definitely should be a psychologist or a social worker," Austin told him.

"No, you must have me confused with Dad," Nate reacted. "He's the one who wants to help others all the time."

"Well, how about a salesman?" Austin asked. "You could make a lot of money."

"Now that sounds like something I could do," Nate said as he smiled charmingly.

During his freshman year, Austin adapted smoothly to the huge university, the rigors of studying, and the requirements for self-sufficiency. He lived for the Saturday football games when enemies Michigan State, Purdue, and the biggest enemy of all—Michigan—invaded the horseshoe-shaped stadium named for legendary Woody Hayes.

During Austin's five years at Ohio State as a student, the football team displayed a kind of power and dominance that served to reaffirm what Austin had grown up believing—that he himself could be or do anything if he tried hard enough.

Late in his freshman year, Austin suffered a major disappointment: his mom broke the news to him that Nate would not be joining him at Ohio State.

"Why not, Mom? Why not?" he asked his mother pleadingly by phone. "And why didn't he have the guts to tell me himself?" he asked somewhat angrily on the heels of his first question.

"Honey, you know Nate has always idolized you, has always wanted to be like you. But you also must know that he isn't. He isn't like you when it comes to his dedication to school."

"But he could be dedicated if he just buckled down a little and tried harder."

"You can believe that if you want to, Austin, but I don't. We all have certain things we're good at and certain things we like to do. Just because you and Nate have the same parents, me and Dad, and just because you grew up in the same family does not mean that you two are alike. You need to be what you are and what you want to be and let Nate be Nate."

Austin reluctantly understood what his mom was saying, but he didn't like it. He just wished Nate could live up to his potential, achieve at higher levels, and come down to Ohio State so they could be together.

Austin, increasingly the devoted Buckeye football fan, figured out ways to go to some of the away games and help the Scarlet and Gray earn their rap as having "bad fans." Never backing down from a fight and sometimes even helping to incite brawls, Austin loved the away games. He found them to be outlets for expressing his anger. No big Ohio State security cops to grab your ID and parlay your misdeeds into academic penalties.

CHAPTER 38

Austin secured the job at the Victory Circle. Lorena Weiss, the owner, let Austin live up above the restaurant for free, knowing that he was the cheapest guard dog she could find. Lorena slept less fitfully at her stately home in Bexley, just on the other side of East Columbus, knowing that Austin was there.

Austin quickly became multicomforting to Lorena, who had lost her husband Len three years earlier. It had been sudden and unexpected. She had read and had been told it would take at least a year for her to get through the grief of losing a spouse. It would be a year before she would start to feel like her old self—the same person, complete with feelings and needs that she had had before Len's death.

Three years after his death, she still had most of the feelings of despair and uselessness that had swept over her the night of Len's departure. He had been her soul mate, the one person who truly accepted her, who believed in her, and who never stayed upset with her. He admired her more than anyone he had ever known and loved her without complications and contingencies. Lorena never wanted to disappoint him.

CHAPTER 39

Lorena had wanted to go with Len when he passed, to join him in death or in whatever life hereafter they might encounter. She shrieked at the funeral (totally uncharacteristic of the reserved, sophisticated lady she had become) and even attempted to climb into the casket with him before it was closed.

But she didn't die, and she didn't join him. Instead, she hung onto the notion that she would try to do in this life, in this world, what Len would have wanted her to do. She and Len had no children, no legacy in the sense of a next generation of survivors upon whom to bestow their values, their beliefs, their good name, and their wealth.

But Lorena knew. She just knew that Len would be so proud of her as she kept racking up profits at the Victory Circle and nearly doubled the worth of the Len and Lorena Weiss Foundation. If he could—and maybe he could—look down and see her, she absolutely knew he would be lovingly proud of her.

When Austin came along, he actually reminded Lorena, in an instant, of Len—confident but unassuming, smart, quick, and charming without even trying to be. He had the same look—handsome, sure of himself, believing that he could have whoever he wanted as an intimate friend—that Len had exuded.

For the first time in three years, Lorena, a fifty-three-year-old widow, had a living man in her dreams—a twenty-year-old seemingly worldly young man from a farm in Northern Ohio. She had instantly hired him to help her at the Victory Circle.

Lorena was curious about Austin and wanted to know everything about him. She wanted to know what his parents were like and what his future goals were. She also seemed fascinated with Nate. "Why is he so different from you? Was one of you adopted?" she once asked, eerily serious.

"Of course not," Austin reacted with a look suggesting that Lorena not be silly. "My psychology professor tells us that genetics is only part of what shapes us into who we are—environment is the other big factor."

"But you both had the same environment. You both grew up with the same mother and father. He just seemed so different from you as soon as I met him."

Lorena had first met Nate when he had accompanied his parents to Columbus for a football game. The three of them were a little confused that Austin had brought his boss, Lorena Weiss, to the game, and then the five of them had gone to the Victory Circle to celebrate a lop-sided final score. They were even further confused by how much Austin admired his boss and "hung onto her every word" and vice versa. They discussed the matter at length driving home to Medina but could not seem to reach some sort of common conclusion.

"Let's just say that Austin and his boss have a kind of relationship that none of us can understand," Mrs. Morris tried to summarize. "Maybe we don't want to dig into it too deeply."

"I don't know. The whole thing makes me uncomfortable," her husband responded critically, shaking his head. "I can't talk to Austin—he always takes my advice as criticism."

"I think he really likes her, maybe sort of loves her," Nate, the admiring younger brother surmised. "He learned a lot from both of you guys. One thing about Austin, he always knows what he is doing," Nate continued as he wondered to himself if his older brother was sleeping with his boss.

CHAPTER 40

During slow times at the restaurant and sometimes after closing, Lorena and Austin would talk and talk without any censorship or self-consciousness. She loved Austin, actually from the start, because he helped her feel about herself just as she had when she had been with Len: pretty on the outside, beautiful on the inside, and valued for her thinking and perceptions. Back with Len and now during times with Austin, Lorena experienced rarified moments during which she felt as if she were the center of the universe.

The five years at Ohio State were awakening, glorious years for Austin. He avidly supported the Buckeyes in spirit and in deed. He attended all the home football games, many of the away games, and all the baseball games. "Somehow, I made the baseball team!" he had excitedly told Nate, then his parents, and then Lorena.

"I'll be playing mostly right field, and I'll bat seventh or eighth in the lineup," he had informed Nate.

"Once they see how far you can hit the ball and how good you are at getting on base, they'll move you to cleanup!" Nate had said encouragingly.

Austin studied accounting in college. He didn't love it, sort of liked it, but seemed to have a real knack for it. A's came with moderate effort; B's came with minimal effort.

Lorena and the Victory Circle gave him all the practical experience he needed, keeping the books and gradually taking on some of the financial responsibilities for Lenlor, the holding company Len had formed for him and Lorena to expand their wealth into diverse areas—apartments, laundromats, storage unit rentals, and stock holdings that focused on Ohio-based companies' stocks.

"Guess what—you can be an intern for me, for Lenlor!" Lorena had told Austin one evening midway through his sophomore year.

"And just what all does that entail or entitle me to?" Austin asked in a cute, semi-flirtatious way.

"It entitles you to be my closest associate and personal assistant," Lorena blushingly responded and with surprising seriousness in her voice. Lorena had gone through the detailed efforts to arrange for a legitimate internship program with Ohio State's business college, knowing that Austin, Lenlor's first intern, would be pleased.

Austin, in addition to living upstairs above the Victory Circle and adding an immeasurable sense of security, provided rejuvenation for Lorena. Little by little, she began to feel like her old self again, like a whole person, just as she had when Len was alive.

She went to bed and looked forward to getting up the next morning. Sometimes she would wake up early in the morning, perhaps four in the morning, and feel warm and excited. She told Austin about her early morning awakenings to which he reacted by asking, "Do you think about me—when you wake up at four in the morning?"

Without a touch of embarrassment, she answered "Well, yes I do. How'd you guess?"

"'Cause I know you and am tuned into you. I've never met anyone like you, and we seem to have complete simpatico. You and I have some of what you and Len had. Some, but of course not all. You and he were the greatest couple, the best friends and loving partners I've ever known of."

"You're right, of course," Lorena murmured.

Austin and Lorena shared their lives together for a solid, wonderful four-year span. Lorena lived with hope and without grief, and Austin lived with hope and with no regrets. They worked together, learned together, and playfully spent time together.

Austin's time away from Lorena was mostly spent around sports—mainly practicing and playing baseball.

Lorena knew very little about baseball and almost inexplicably had no interest in learning. Although well-versed on most subjects and generally considerably curious, Lorena never sought to understand the game. She was, of course, very interested in Austin's experience and feelings with regard to practice, games, fellow players, and coaches, but that was the extent of her interest.

"I'm not sure of the basis for my indifference toward the game," she said apologetically more than once to Austin. "Maybe it's the slowness of the game or how time-consuming it feels when I watch a game. I sort of sit and watch and tune out, which can cause me to drift toward thoughts I don't like."

"I understand. It's no problem," Austin would respond. And he didn't mind at all. He appreciated having a facet of his life that was his own, within which he had some privacy from Lorena. Not that he didn't like their closeness and their blending of life's interests and activities.

He didn't want Lorena to do anything that she didn't want to do (although he already knew that she wouldn't). His space with regard to baseball served as an ongoing yet unnecessary affirmation that they each were free to be themselves to do as they wanted, all as part of the relationship.

Austin treasured their relationship and felt that practically nothing could hurt it or taint it. He was careful, however, not to talk about the occasional coed he would go out with, thinking that it might, in some way, upset Lorena. He especially wanted to avoid talking about Sasha, his girlfriend "on the side" who faithfully attended every baseball game and many of the practices.

"I love our relationship." Austin was effusive in telling Lorena. "It's incredible how close we have become and how we can tell each other everything."

"Well, mostly I guess," Lorena responded. "Certainly everything that is necessary to be known."

"What do you mean by that? Are you holding something back?" the young man asked.

"If I am holding back anything, it is not important. Not important to us or for our relationship," the wiser, more life-seasoned lady stated. "None of us should tell another person everything—some of the things about me, my past, my relationship with Len are not important for you to know. They are simply past experiences and have very little to do with who I am. Sometimes the past is hardly a memory."

"But I want to know you, to know everything about you," Austin asserted, almost pleadingly, although at the same time feeling justified in his not discussing with Lorena his occasional dates with coeds or his stormy relationship with Sasha.

"You do know me, probably as well as anybody possibly could. Knowing every little thing about me would not help you know me any better or any deeper. Besides, you never really know anyone completely," she told him.

"But *I* do," he told her.

"No, you only *think* you do."

And so a discussion began about how well one person can know another or even hope to know another.

"We never know what we would do if we were in someone's exact situation," Lorena expounded. "We see an old person refusing medical treatment, perhaps chemo, and we ask, 'How could she do that?' but we never know what we would do if we were in the exact same circumstances. Life and other things probably look different to an eighty-year-old from they do to a forty-year-old."

"I've learned a lot about people in the psych courses I've taken," Austin asserted, not giving up his point of view.

"That's true. You have. And you have a good, natural 'feel' for people too."

Austin wanted to believe that what he and Lorena had was as close to a perfect relationship as any two people, other than Lorena and Len, could have. He wanted to believe that she shared everything openly and completely with him, either volunteered or in response to questions. He didn't like the idea of her withholding information, although admittedly, he did some withholding of his own. But he wanted to be the one to decide what information or what experiences from Lorena's past were important for him to know.

Chapter 41

There was no strife, no rivalry, no negative possessiveness in the relationship of Austin Morris and Lorena Weiss. They were two travelers joined on a journey; though time-limited, neither wondered about when the journey would end. Nor did either worry about the destination.

But Austin wanted to know more about her and her past—what did she think about at baseball games as her mind drifted that caused her distress?

It was Austin's senior year, actually his fifth year, at Ohio State.

It was a Saturday afternoon, midafternoon, and the Buckeyes had an away football game at Indiana. Austin had chosen not to go. The Victory Circle was fairly dead as many of the college students were in Bloomington, drinking and rooting for their only team of choice.

As frequently was the case, Lorena looked at Austin, and he nodded. She asked with her eyes if he wanted to leave, to get out of the pizza parlor, and he responded affirmatively.

As soon as Austin got behind the wheel of Lorena's massive Mercedes, he suspected they were coming to the end of their journey together.

It had been a significant four-year period together—best friends, adoring admirers, and yes, soul mates. Neither was incomplete, but each was even more complete with the other.

The difference in age was physically noticeable but psychologically indistinguishable. They both seemed to come together someplace in the middle, say, around forty years of age. They even referred to their relationship, their combined "being," as "forever forty."

When people saw them together, they were briefly quizzical but then soon seemed to understand. A few jibes or irreverent comments were made and sometimes regretted. Comments such as "I wonder if that young guy

---

is servicing the old broad for her money" or referents such as "Oedipal Austin" or "Sugar Momma" had occasionally sounded within earshot of Austin and Lorena.

Austin and Lorena did not let such comments bother them. They were disarmingly straightforward in professing their friendship and admiration for each other. Many people wondered what went on behind closed doors, but few, if any, really cared. Almost everyone, including Austin's family, had come to respect the relationship and considered it one of those ideal relationships that is found only in fictional descriptions.

CHAPTER 42

Without looking toward her, Austin asked, "How bad is it?" as he aggressively stepped on the gas pedal to lurch from the garage, cross High Street and head east.

"Well, it's not good."

"What can I do?" he asked as he turned to look at her.

He saw a beautiful person, age lines softened, hair thick and naturally streaked with gray. He saw a face he had kissed and a middle-aged woman he had comforted.

He saw the goodness of his mother, of his high school sweetheart, and of all persons feminine whom he had respected and loved. He saw some of Sasha but tried to keep the images separate. Sasha was a sex machine, and he didn't want to think about having sex when he looked at Lorena.

He saw in Lorena none of the pettiness or self-serving qualities he tried to steer away from—whether within a female or a male.

He saw hope and continuation, although he knew that such visions were not to be within the mortal Lorena. This part of their journey together was to be forever changed.

CHAPTER 43

Austin didn't wheel the bulky yet somewhat nimble black Mercedes into the Bexley Monk restaurant as he so frequently had done in the past because he knew Lorena had a lot to tell him, and he knew just the place.

Another five minutes and they were through the front door, the parlor, past the dining room and kitchen, through the family room and onto the back patio—surrounded on both sides by high shrubbery, and to the south by a brick wall identical to the massive veneers of the three-story mansion. Len had added the wall soon after they had purchased the house at a cost that was nearly as much as a small house in Bexley south of Main Street. He had found an old-world caliber brick mason who was successful in removing and cleaning the bricks from a nearby house Lenlor Holdings was refurbishing.

Len had bought the house primarily for its brick—brick that were identical to those in his recently acquired mansion at the time, or "big house" as Len called it. He and Lorena knew the bricks would make a perfect wall for their patio space.

"In the car, you asked what you could do," Lorena said softly.

Austin paused, and they silently communicated.

"Len is all I ever wanted until there was you. Austin, you have been everything, simply everything to me these last four years."

Austin cleared his throat and spoke from a place deep inside. "Lorena, I have never met anyone like you, and I never will."

"I think you will. I *hope* you will."

"I don't know if that's possible. I don't think I will ever find someone as perfect for me as you are."

"That's what I said when Len passed away. I said I'd never meet someone who could measure up to him. I went through all the anger, denial, and so on, and I think I just got stuck at the bitterness stage."

Austin held her close to him, both deriving and imparting strength.

She continued, "That was until I met you. You did it for me. You gave me back my life, my stay of execution. Had it not been for you, I probably wouldn't have lived another four years."

"Of course, you would have!" he insisted through watery eyes.

"Had my life continued, I know I couldn't have lived the life I've known, the life we've known, if it hadn't been for you."

"You know that everything you're saying, I feel exactly the same way."

"You do, but we're looking at this world differently. Although we talk of being "forever forty," we both know we're not. I've been there, want to believe I'm still there, but in reality, chronologically, I'm a good fifteen-plus years on the other side of forty."

"How much time do we have?" he asked.

"We have all the time we need. I never know if I truly believe in a life hereafter, but I fantasize that I will soon rejoin Len. Somehow, I believe he is somewhere waiting for me and that he approves of what I want to do."

"What is it you want to do?" he sobbed.

"I want you to listen, Austin, as I have a proposal to make and a number of things to tell you. If you go along with my plan, we will focus on it and not on my illness. We will live our lives with as much joy as possible. Do you think you can go along with my plan?"

"Sure, Lorena, anything you want. Absolutely anything. What's your plan?" he asked, feeling grief, anxiety, and excitement all at the same time.

"I want you to marry me, Austin," the pretty lady said.

CHAPTER 44

They talked well into the night and without much debate. Austin knew that Lorena was a remarkable woman—intelligent, creative, caring, and above all, strong. He, and probably Len before him, had always recognized these qualities and had quickly evolved a relationship with her that respected all her exceptional qualities and freedoms. Most of all, a freedom to do as she wanted. Respect for this freedom only seemed like the ultimate respect to accord a woman so richly deserving. The only freedom for her that he objected to was her keeping some of her past hidden from him.

When he stared at her, particularly that night just before she drifted to sleep, he saw a sadness in her, a longing in her for something that wasn't to be. Had she done something wrong with Len, perhaps cheated on him? Maybe once, but Austin couldn't imagine Lorena, with all her purity and loving devotion to Len, ever cheating on him.

Lorena had only a few months to live, and she wanted Austin to have everything. She had completed her will with Allan Federer, the Weiss's personal attorney as well as board member of Lenlor. Allan had come up with the idea that Lorena and Austin get married in order to simplify and make the transfer of wealth from her estate to Austin less challengeable.

There were no anticipated challenges to the will, yet anything that Federer's law firm touched, particularly if Allan himself was involved, was virtually bulletproof. Any letter signed by Allan was said to be worth several thousand dollars. A small man but a giant intimidator, Allan's pleasantly worded letters spoke volumes of threat, and most recipients were well-advised to begin peace talks or some type of out-of-court settlement immediately.

much for him; he wanted to make her last days here as positive, perhaps even joyful, as possible.

The one question he had wanted to ask his mom but hadn't was still bothering him. He had come close to asking her but was too embarrassed. What if Lorena expected him to make love to her after they got married?

The other question he was asking himself but dreaded the answer was "How would he break the news to Sasha?"

CHAPTER 47

Austin hadn't known much about Sasha, but he had hired her anyway. As manager of the Victory Circle, one of his main jobs was to hire and fire the servers—the "wait staff" as they were labeled. In the restaurant business, he had begun to conclude that many people were "itinerant workers" passing through, putting in some time until they could find something better.

The kitchen boss, Lorenzo, was different. Lorenzo had landed at the Victory Circle twenty years ago and was hired somewhat out of pity by Len Weiss.

"The boss hired me when I didn't know which end was up," Lorenzo said, never referring to Len Weiss by anything other than "the boss."

"He gave me a job, an opportunity after my wife ran off with a drummer boy and left me with a four-month old. He's done growed up now and playing for the Pittsburg Steelers.

"I never let her back in my life, but she wanted to come home after the drummer boy got tired of her. LeSean, our son, finally let her back in his life after he got famous and started making the big bucks. I guess he forgave her, but I never did. LeSean says everything happens for a reason, but I don't believe it the way he does. I think she left cuz she was a whore."

CHAPTER 48

"You may want to take a look at this honey, Sasha Rinaldi," Lorenzo spoke in a manner that indicated Austin would find her hot and sexy.

"Why? What's she got going for her?" Austin reacted with an innocent face that he knew Lorenzo would know was feigned.

"Man, she's laid out like a granite counter top—firm, full of depth, and waiting to be mounted!"

Austin liked Lorenzo a lot and enjoyed his descriptions of women, oftentimes comparing them to aspects of kitchen environments. "That woman treated me like a portable dishwasher—every time I turned around, she was licking me, clicking me, cleaning me, and loading me to use again."

Sashi Rinaldi was not very tall, but she seemed to think she was. She was bubbly, friendly, a little bit nervous, but never hesitated to take charge of a situation.

"Mr. Morris, I'm Sasha Rinaldi. It's very nice to meet you!" the dark, black-haired, self-possessed beauty spoke. He suspected, and she later confirmed that her father was Italian and her mother was a lady of color.

"Please, call me Austin," he responded, noticing that there seemed to be no barriers to intimacy between them.

He knew instantly that he wanted to have sex with her, but he wanted her to have the same desire with regard to him. He never liked to have one-sided sex; he wanted the other person to want and enjoy it as much as he did.

"No problem, Austin. I really want to work here, you know. I'm friendly, I've got experience, and I'm a people person."

"Have you ever worked in the restaurant business?" he asked, thinking about his nongranite countertop upstairs. No, the bed would be better—at least to get started.

"For sure, my uncle has a subshop in New Jersey, in Morristown. I worked there two summers in a row. I wanted to work in one of the cafeterias here at Ohio State, but my schedule is so crazy, I can't sign up for a steady shift. I never knew I'd have to work in college, but my boyfriend—well, he's not really my boyfriend, we just live together with friends' benefits—says I need to work at least twenty-five hours a week, mostly at night."

She communicated in a rush of words then with another and another. Austin was drawn to her and was already concluding that her boobs, big and hard, were man-made. She had a kind of unrefined air of sophistication and seemed to operate without much self-censorship. Sasha conveyed excitement.

"I grew up as a princess. If I had been Jewish, I'd have been a JAP. But being black Italian, I guess I was spoiled and placed on a pedestal by my dad and my uncle. Everybody said Daddy was in the Mafia, but I don't know . . . He always kept guns around, but he didn't use 'em, at least not as far as I knew . . ."

Her voice trailed off and seemed to invite questions. Before Austin could ask a question, though, she started another word rush.

"I never thought I'd be working in college cuz Daddy set aside plenty of money for me and my brother. I have an older brother, but he didn't come way the fuck out here—oops, excuse me—he went to Rutgers and then Seton Hall for a while. He made fun of me going all the way out to the Midwest, to Ohio, and said I'd regret it. He pissed me off, but I love him. I just think I gotta be strong and independent, and I told my whole family that I'm a survivor. I don't want to be dependent on them and their money, so I said once they paid my tuition, I'd pay the rest. That's room, board, and spending money. But now I'm really low on capital, and I need to work *because I can't* go crawling home and ask for money. I'm too proud," she insisted, punctuating her assertion by sitting up even straighter and jutting out her breasts even further.

CHAPTER 49

Soon after Sasha began working at the Victory Circle, Austin found an opportunity to invite her upstairs.

"You want to see where I live?" he asked her on a slow Saturday afternoon. It was an away football game weekend, and Lorena was home, sick with some sort of viral infection or flu bug. "Timing is everything," Austin said to himself.

"Absolutely!" Sasha responded and suddenly emitted a glow and an alluring aroma.

The aroma smelled like sex to Austin, which turned him on immediately, and he tried to hide his private reaction. Sasha looked down and smiled. She was pleased.

"I'm glad Ms. L isn't here, aren't you?" she asked with a flirtatious look.

"What do you mean? Lorena's home with the flu or something."

Austin wanted to correct Sasha and request that she call Lorena by her given name, but he was not direct. He knew that Lorena preferred to be called Lorena or Mrs. Weiss and really didn't like to be called Ms. L.

"I see the way she looks at you, Austin. Everyone does—it's sort of like a mother hen, protective and all. It's also sort of creepy, like a mother or father that wants to have sex with one of their own. Like—well, you know."

"You're crazy." Austin laughed, trying to shrug it off and change the subject. "She's my mentor—she and I are not sexually attracted to each other."

"Speak for yourself, big fella," she retorted, once again looking with desire at the bulging area just below his belt buckle and speaking as if there were another separate person within his pants.

"I'm not like you, Sasha—I don't have sex with someone just because we're friends. I only have sex with people I care about and only if they care about me too."

She knew he was making a dig about Anthony, her roommate. He had never asked much about Anthony, but for whatever reason, she had told him almost everything about Anthony and their relationship. Almost. She hadn't told him that Anthony was very much in love with her and wanted to marry her.

Sasha, on the other hand, really liked Anthony as a friend but could not see being married to him—at least for now.

Her father liked Anthony but did not like the idea of his daughter and Anthony being roommates. Sasha and Anthony both swore to her father that theirs was a completely platonic relationship and that they had never done *anything*.

Mr. Rinaldi was ultimately sold on the idea of Anthony being her roommate when his glamorous (and possibly vulnerable) daughter had said she felt safe with Anthony around.

"He's my protection, Daddy. He would kill anybody who ever tried to hurt me. You know he keeps guns in the apartment and carries one with him whenever he can."

Mr. Rinaldi had watched Anthony handle a couple of different models from his own gun collection and could tell right away that Anthony was no novice.

CHAPTER 50

The stairs seemed long and steep to Austin. Maybe he was just in a hurry to get inside and get busy. Clearly, Sasha wanted to savor the moment and seemed oblivious to everything—except for Austin.

Once inside, with the door securely bolted, she turned and focused totally on him. She pressed him firmly, passionately, and kept pulling his neck and head down toward her. Austin realized how short she was, especially when compared to him.

She opened her mouth widely but kept her lips tightly connected to his. She inhaled through his mouth and sucked the air from him. He knew what it felt like to be possessed.

"Let's see if we can find a bed, big guy." She grabbed his belt underneath the buckle and aggressively tugged him.

He guided her backward through the unnoticed kitchen and dining area, the length of the hallway past the dark bathroom to the single bedroom at the rear of the apartment. *Thank God*, he thought, *the sheets were fairly clean and the covers were not in disarray.* Clearly, none of this registered with Sasha because nothing other than making love with Austin mattered at all.

She pulled him on top of her as one and then fell backward onto the queen-size bed almost acrobatically. She seemed so small to Austin in the oversized bed, but his visual observations lessened, except for very up-close ones.

CHAPTER 51

Sasha and Austin had, for a while, what seemed like a perfect relationship. It wasn't very deep, and it was mostly about sex. He made few demands on her, and she made none on him.

Except for sex.

"Austin, can we slip upstairs for a quickie before I go home tonight?"

"I don't know. Lorena wants me to come out to her house tonight and meet some of her friends."

"You don't want to be with a bunch of old farts, do you?"

"Not as much as I want to be with you," Austin responded sincerely. He didn't really like it when Sasha made fun of Lorena, calling her Ms. L or referring to her as being old or over the hill.

But he didn't say much, partly because he could understand how a vibrant young girl like Sasha would see anybody over thirty as at least middle aged. And partly, he didn't want to jeopardize his readily available supply of incredible sex.

"You think everybody's old, and maybe they are—compared to you," he said.

"Well, I know you think my development has been arrested at the adolescent stage of development. You guys who take a psych course go around diagnosing the rest of us innocents," she cooed.

"Well, maybe . . ." They both knew what the other wanted.

"You need to let yourself go, Austin, and do what you want," Sasha said forcefully. "That's my job—to get you to quit being so stodgy, so serious for your age. I know Lorena is your boss and a nice enough lady, I guess, but you don't have to cater to everything she wants. Tell her you're gonna be tied up tonight, with some pressing assignment," she said as she pressed her hard little body with her man-made breasts closely against him near the bar.

"Sasha, be careful! What if somebody sees you?"

"Who? Lorena's home—you told me."

"Like maybe a customer. We don't want the Victory Circle to be seen as a place where the manager or the wait staff are on the make."

"But I *am* on the make—for you!" She grabbed his testicles for added (but gentle) emphasis.

"What about if Anthony comes in?"

"Anthony's not coming in here. I've told him not to. I don't want him all worried and jealous."

"But you told me you weren't in love with each other, that you lived together with 'friends' benefits."

She paused for once before reacting.

"We do have friends' benefits, and I don't love him, but he does seem to love me."

Austin could understand loving Sasha, although he was convinced he himself didn't love her.

But he loved making love to her. He had never had sex with anyone that even came close to what it was with Sasha. They were totally compatible in the bedroom from head to toe and every place in between.

"How's my big Audie?" she would say whenever she reached into his pants to pull out his seemingly always hard penis. She had asked Austin the first time they had made love what his name for his penis was.

"I've never named him," he confessed honestly.

"Then you won't mind if I name him," she said as she licked his lips and then gently licked the head of his penis.

He groaned, which apparently, she took as an affirmative.

"Okay then. I think I'll name him Audie."

As she pressed against him again, he was brought back to the reality of the moment.

"Okay, lover. I'll call our boss and tell her I'll be an hour or so late," he said as he surrendered.

CHAPTER 52

"Sasha, I need to tell you something," Austin said with hesitation in his voice.

"What's wrong?" the pixie-like, black-haired lovemaker asked.

Her eyes were big, her mind always raced, and Austin knew this was not going to be easy.

"Sweetie, I have some good news and some bad news."

"Don't give me that shit. That's always bullshit!" Rage was a terrible thing, Austin acknowledged to himself. He was always baffled by her instantaneous mood swings, particularly when her mood was headed toward rage.

"Now don't get pissed—"

"Don't tell me not to get pissed—that means you know I will be! Just tell me the fucking truth! You've been acting strange, really weird since you went up to see your parents. What'd they do, tell you to kick your black dago girlfriend to the curb?"

"No, no, no, it's not about them—it's about Lorena."

He was now doubting whether he could really tell Sasha that he had agreed to marry Lorena.

"What's wrong with that old bitch? Is she gonna die?"

Jesus, he thought . . . Was he that transparent?

"Well, as a matter of fact, she is—but you gotta promise not to say anything. Don't tell anybody at the VC, and don't send any signals to Lorena that you know. It would ruin everything."

Sasha was fuming, wondering what he *wasn't* telling her. She was scared, thinking that what they had going as an intimate couple was about to go away, to be destroyed. She felt herself imploding . . .

"Wait a minute," she said, thinking to herself that she wished her dad was here. He would know what to do—maybe he'd kill Austin or at least shoot him. At the very least, he'd cold-cock him.

"You said good news, bad news—what the fuck's the good news?"

"Well . . ." He paused, and she knew he was holding back.

"The good news is that after she passes, you and I will have more time together. We can come out of hiding and let the world know that we're dating."

"Dating?" she responded incredulously. "You mean *fucking!* We've never been out on a real date. You've never held my hand in public. You've kept me a prisoner so you can fuck me—F-U-C-K me!"

"Why are you so upset, honey?" He reached for her, but she pushed him hard with both hands in the chest. She was filled with anger and revenge.

Austin wasn't giving up . . . "But we will have money—you don't understand. Lorena is putting me in her will and is going to leave me a ton of money. We can be happy. We can come out of the bedroom and be a couple."

Suddenly, Sasha began to cry. Softly at first, pitifully, and then as one who had just lost the love of her life.

"Wait, honey." Austin reached for her and touched her. But her skin, her body showed no yielding. She was pulling back, and every fiber within her was trying to shut him out.

"Why are you pulling back from me, Sasha?"

"Don't you see, Austin? You are destroying a perfect relationship. Our relationship is based on our natural, spontaneous love for each other. Our bodies love each other. We don't worry about getting to know each other. We don't try to change each other. You are you, and I am me. We come together and become one. Our bodies take on a single existence—that's why we can fuck all night long. It's like a power from the universe. Every other relationship in my life is mundane and boring. They are filled with details and human, crummy feelings. Explanations—why did you do this, or why did you do that?"

"We can overcome all that, Sasha. Don't you see? Don't you want to try and make it as a couple?" Austin pleaded.

"No, I don't. I love what we have, and now you're gonna change it. You already have."

Sasha was crying softly, vowing to herself to let go of the rage and to let go of Austin.

"I haven't changed it—damn! You're all pissed because Lorena's going to die, and somehow, it's going to make our relationship like everybody else's."

"I understand, Austin, and I'm done."

"Please don't leave me, Sasha. I love you!"

"You think you love me, and maybe you do. You love having sex with me, but love is more than sex. I don't know if I love you or not, even though I've told you I do, especially during orgasms."

"Don't you want to give it a try for Christ's sake? I know we can take what we have to the next level." Austin was tearing up, actually crying, and actually begging.

"I don't know if I want to go to the next level with you. I don't think I can."

"Why not?"

Austin felt a strange resurgence of hope. It felt extremely good, perhaps like what the convicted prisoner feels when given a stay of execution, he suddenly thought to himself.

"Because I know there's a bunch of shit about Lorena—stuff that's gone on between you two that I don't like. You've got all kinds of baggage with her, and once she dies, it's all going to come out, and you're going to have to deal with it. I don't think I can be there or even want to be there for you to help you through all the shit."

"I don't know what you mean—Jesus, Sasha!"

"Let me be blunt, Austin. You and she have been having some kind of affair for years. Just like Anthony and me. I'm hiding mine from my parents. You're probably hiding yours from your parents. I know we're hiding our feelings for Lorena and Anthony from each other."

"You mean you're in love with Anthony? I thought it was only one-sided and just for friends' benefits."

"I don't know what it is, Austin, but I know this—you are more than friends with Lorena. She's more than a mentor. She's what you want your future wife to look like and be like, only thirty years younger! You're probably fucking her, and I don't care! But once she dies, I don't want to help you try to figure out what happened—was I in love with her or was I a prostitute, being nice to her or whatever so I could get a bunch of her money? I'm tired, I'm done, and I quit. Find somebody else, but you'll never find somebody as good as me. You'll probably never understand that we had a perfect relationship, and you, yes YOU, fucked it up!"

"Wait, Sasha—"

But she didn't.

CHAPTER 53

Austin spent most of that night in pain, wondering why Sasha had left. He texted her several times, but she didn't respond. He hadn't even told her the worst thing—that he was going to marry Lorena before she died.

That would sort of justify his inheriting her money.

No, maybe that would just verify that he was a prostitute. But he knew, or thought he knew, in his heart that he was a good person and was not using Lorena.

She was the one who wanted him to marry her. It was *her* idea; he was just trying to help her during a critical time of need.

He knew that fairly soon, Sasha would find out about the wedding. Maybe he should be the one to tell her before she found out in some other way.

Maybe Sasha was right—that theirs was a perfect relationship and that other relationships were encumbered with self-centeredness and each person taking turns trying to change the other one.

He would call Sasha tomorrow and, if necessary, go and find her.

CHAPTER 54

Clearly, Sasha was avoiding him. He tried calling, leaving messages, texting, and driving by her house.

Finally, that night, he found himself sitting in the dark in Columbus's Short North District, waiting to try to tell Sasha face-to-face about the upcoming wedding. Maybe she would understand. He knew she wouldn't agree with his decision and his thinking behind it, but maybe she would give him a little bit of time and, eventually, another chance.

He wasn't sure how to say it or how to lead into it. Given her anger yesterday, which knowing her, probably hadn't dissipated, he thought he would just make their interaction short and sweet. But he would add a comment about loving her and someday trying to reconnect.

He had thought about her comments from yesterday . . . Maybe they did have a perfect relationship. Maybe they didn't really know much about each other's pasts, and certainly, they were not about trying to change each other.

One thing was for sure—their lovemaking, their sex, was extreme. He knew, or thought he knew, he would never find someone who could turn him on again and again and again like Sasha could.

Every time they had sex, it was like the first time all over again. But better.

He absolutely did not want to even think about the possibility of losing his luscious, marathon sex partner.

CHAPTER 55

Suddenly, he saw Sasha's little green convertible whip into the space two cars in front of him.

Eagerly, he jumped out to catch her but realized she was not alone.

Anthony! She had Anthony with her, stretching out of the passenger's side and to the sidewalk. He was bigger than he had appeared to be in the one or two pictures Austin had seen of him. Sasha must have stood on her tiptoes in one of their pictures together, posing happily for whoever the picture taker was.

In a flash, Austin concluded that Anthony was not going to be aggressive and come after him. Austin sensed that he wasn't afraid of fighting (nor was he) but that there would be no need. Anthony had won Sasha, and his calm half-smile conveyed the confidence that went with his victory.

"Austin, what the fuck are you doing here? This is Anthony—Anthony, this is Austin." Sasha seemed irritated, not totally pissed, and at some level, pleased or flattered that Austin had shown up.

"I just wanted to see you and tell you I was sorry about yesterday."

Thinking quickly and assuming that Sasha had quit her job at the VC, Austin added, "And I wanted you to reconsider coming back to work at the Victory Circle."

"Anthony, you can go inside and wait for me. I need to tell Austin why I won't be coming back."

Anthony beamed at her knowingly, gave her a quick, supportive, and surprisingly gentle hug, and left the two of them on the sidewalk without looking back. Austin fleetingly wondered if Sasha had named Anthony's penis also—maybe "Tony."

"Sasha, I don't want you to leave me, and we can get through this. I didn't tell you yesterday, but I agreed to marry Lorena very soon before she dies."

Austin was dumbfounded by her lack of reaction.

"Once she dies, you and I can go anyplace and do anything we want."

Sasha shook her head slowly and glared at him. He didn't sense hatred, but he sensed that she didn't like him anymore. How could she get over him so quickly?

"Look, Austin. We had a thing, maybe a perfect thing, but not anymore. We both have to move on. I'm not surprised you're gonna marry the old lady for her money. Everything happens for a reason, and I think I know now that I love Anthony. He's more than a buddy or a sex partner—he's a guy I may want to spend my life with. You taking an old lady's money and now you tell me you're going to marry her—I don't respect you anymore. And I certainly don't want to give you my body anymore. Please remember what we had but forget about me. Don't argue. Don't talk to me anymore. Just leave me the fuck alone! If you ever really cared about me, show me now by letting me go. Please—leave me alone!"

She was ice cold and turned to walk away. Austin started to reach for her but then didn't.

He knew she meant what she said but hoped it might change. Probably, Anthony was better suited for her than he was. They had history, and maybe they would have a future.

He hurriedly jumped into the black Mercedes and pressed "1" to let Lorena know he was on his way and would be on time for the in-home visit by Mr. Mangini, whose specialty was quick turnarounds on tailored formal wear.

Lorena was buying him a tux, one of her several wedding gifts for him.

CHAPTER 56

The wedding was very small, very solemn, and attended by Austin's mom, dad, and best man Nate. Allan Federer and his wife were there to witness the exchange of vows between the young man and older woman.

The ceremony was performed by Rabbi Stuart Lieberman, who had been a childhood friend of Lorena's in Shaker Heights, a suburb of Cleveland. Rabbi Lieberman had a thick shock of gray and black hair combed straight back and thinned by his stylist to better accommodate his perennial yarmulke.

Both Austin and Lorena felt good as they pledged their commitments to each other. The cloth-wrapped wineglass shattered from one decisive stomp by Austin, and the two became Mr. and Mrs. Austin Morris.

A simple meal was served at the big house in Bexley, and the newlyweds were whisked away by limo to Lenlor's hangar at the Columbus airport. The Gulfstream was waiting to take them to Boca Raton, Florida.

"Do you feel married?" Lorena asked the next morning as they looked at the ocean from their penthouse balcony.

"I guess I do. I'm not really sure," Austin said.

He looked admiringly at his wife's firm middle-aged body clad in a relatively skimpy swimsuit. He wanted to comfort her and to make her every moment as pleasurable as possible. If he were to develop any doubts about what he had done, he would not allow them to encroach upon their happiness together.

"That's true," his new wife responded. "But when you've had a truly wonderful marriage, you don't want it to end—you just want to extend it. I'm very glad we're married, and I'm much more at peace than if I were going through the next few months alone."

Maybe getting married wasn't just a way of keeping some of her wealth away from the government, Austin thought. She was so happy being married to Len that she wanted to be married again and to leave this life as a married woman.

She was so calm, so relaxed, that Austin wondered if there might be some other motive behind her wanting him to marry her. Her peace of mind was striking and made him wonder.

Austin enjoyed their short honeymoon and found comfort in fulfilling Lorena's needs.

CHAPTER 57

The shock of Lorena's death was very difficult for Austin. It came exactly three months after their wedding. Although anticipated, it felt very premature. He supposed that no matter the circumstances, the surviving loved one wishes the departed one could have waited just a little bit longer.

He could not find comfort in the fact that she had gone quickly and with minimal pain.

Nor could he find comfort in the fact that they had not consummated the marriage sexually. He sensed that she wanted to make love, but she had never asked, and he had never offered.

PART IV

CHAPTER 58

On the same midsummer evening that Angela had gone out with Kenny on her sixteenth birthday, over two hundred miles north in a suburban Cleveland home, a family was sitting shivah, mourning the loss of husband and father Harry Rosen. His wife Elinor, pale white with a dated blond bubble-cut enlarged by an inexpensive weave, was unable to sit without twitching.

"Mother, you know you'll be all right, don't you? Daddy left you with plenty of stocks and savings, didn't he?" The thirty-six-year-old Janie Rosen, devoted daughter and only child, tried her best to be helpful, to be supportive.

Janie knew her mother was emotionally fragile, had a difficult time confronting her feelings, and instead preferred to assure others blandly and nonconvincingly. "I'll be fine," which, at the moment, was how Elinor responded to Janie. "But, Mother, you know this is going to be a period of adjustment, a very difficult period for all of us."

"Please don't worry about me, Jane," Elinor reacted with a pained look on her face as if she had suddenly been surprised by a sour taste.

"I'm not really worried," Janie responded, trying to be soothing while wondering why her mother had always insisted on calling her Jane instead of Janie. When she had unofficially changed her name to Janie in the sixth grade to try to quell classmates' taunts of "Plain Jane," she had begged her mother to switch to Janie, especially when teachers and classmates made the shift.

"I've tried, Jane, but you'll always be Jane to me," her mother had finally said with a sad kind of resignation.

But Harry, her dad, had no trouble calling her Janie. He always did whatever he could to please his little daughter, one of many so-called Jewish American Princesses in the Shaker Heights-Beachwood area.

Janie loved her dad and always called him daddy. He was her biggest fan, her biggest advocate, and always took her side against his wife.

"Let the girl grow up for God's sake, Elinor!" he would say with a thick layer of disapproval aimed at his wife.

For many years, Janie enjoyed this kind of automatic support, this unconditional love, and this approval from her dad. But when she was barely a teenager, her thinking dramatically shifted. She had found her mother alone in her room on many occasions, crying, actually sobbing softly. Janie believed her mother did not really want to be discovered.

"Mother, what's wrong?" she would ask on these occasions but never received complete answers. But Janie was very smart, knew a great deal about people, and had an insatiable curiosity about psychology ever since having read Calvin Hall's *A Primer of Freudian Psychology* at age twelve.

Janie received bits and pieces, snippets of sorts from her mother when queried about her crying. "I have not been a good mother, Jane, and I know you must believe that. I've let your father overpower me and become domineering with you and how you are being raised. You know he's not always correct, and sometimes the things he has done with you have been bad, very bad."

CHAPTER 59

At first, Janie thought her mother was referring to the times her father had overridden her mother's advice or decisions. "If Janie wants to have a sleepover, I think it's okay, Elinor. Just because you've always been an introvert without many friends, you're not going to turn my daughter into the same thing."

Janie found herself in a very uncomfortable, tenuous triangle. As she gained strength and power, her mother lost equivalent amounts. If her mother made a decision Janie didn't like, her dad would reverse the decision, praise his daughter, and put down his wife in one angry swoop.

As a teenager, Janie found herself protecting her mother from her dad, sometimes defending her mother even though she might be at odds with her mother.

"No, I agree with Mother, Daddy. I think I should get an SUV for my birthday because it is safer than the sports car you and I test drove." Or later, "No, Daddy. I think I should stay in the area and go to Case Western Reserve. Maybe when I go to medical school or law school, I will go someplace out of town."

"I never did enough to protect you Jane, and I'll never forgive myself," her mother had told her on the one afternoon Janie had found her especially distraught.

"Protect me from what?" Janie was irritated and really wanted to know.

"Oh, Jane. You don't know? Maybe I'm crazy!"

"Mother—protect me from what?" Janie demanded.

"From your father, you poor thing! He'll kill me if he ever finds out I've told you—but I caught him in your room at nights when you were in the second grade, doing things he never should have done!" Elinor had

133

a crazed look of fiery fear in her eyes, and Janie didn't know whether to believe she knew what she was talking about or not.

"You mean, like *touching* me, Mother?" she asked, with a calmness that surprised them both.

"Oh, God, forgive me, but *yes*. He was sick. He is sick, but I've tried to watch you like a hawk and keep him away from you, especially at night. If I sleep at all, it's very, very lightly. If your father makes the slightest move in the bed at night, I wake up."

"But, Mother, I don't remember this at all. Do you think you could possibly be imagining this?"

"No, I'm not imagining it. I've read that people repress traumas like this. They put a cover on them and bury them and try to go on with a normal life. But if you study psychiatry or if you get into therapy, you might take the lid off this and remember."

Elinor seemed confident of her opinion, but Janie believed her mother was wrong. Maybe not crazy, but wrong.

CHAPTER 60

Janie Rosen never went to medical school or law school; instead, she attended the graduate school of social work at Case Western Reserve University. She had compiled an excellent undergrad record at Case yet had built up considerable ambivalence about leaving Cleveland. She did not want to leave the small, tightly-knit East Side Jewish community in which she had grown up. Her father's health was rapidly failing, and he was recuperating at Mt. Sinai Hospital from a second stroke.

Her father, though not totally himself, continued to adore his only daughter and gave her an impassioned "My princess!" greeting as she walked into his hospital room. She had seen her mother outside in the smoking area on her way into the building, but her mother had not seen her.

Avoiding or keeping a minimum interaction with her mother seemed like a good way to go. Janie had eventually started therapy and had spent many sessions with her therapist, Dr. Edberg, discussing her mother and possible toxic influences of both parents.

"Clearly, you and your father spent some time ganging up on your mother," Dr. Edberg had reflected.

"And we took away what little power in the family she once had," Janie asserted.

"Perhaps, but I doubt that was anybody's overt intention," he suggested, although Janie knew her father wanted to keep her mother in a submissive role.

"Maybe I had this Electra complex thing going with my father, you know, the thing where a daughter wants to be with her father and cut the mother out of the loop."

"Maybe you did . . ."

"But I still don't think Daddy ever molested me," Janie spoke with certainty.

"It's readily apparent that you have no memory of such," Dr. Edberg added supportively.

"But this attraction to my father might have something to do with my numerous failed relationships with men."

"We've talked about many of those relationships, and I'm going to make a note to pick those up next time. I'll see you next week?"

"Sure. Thank you." Janie stood up abruptly and left his office through the side exit door. Neither she nor Dr. Edberg wanted her to see another patient who might be sitting in the waiting area just inside the entry door.

The therapy sessions always seemed to end abruptly for Janie. "I just start to get into some good stuff or to tie some things together when the therapy session ends," she had said aloud to herself more than once.

"That's why some therapists say the most important part of a therapy session is the final ten minutes," her supervising professor, Mildred Lewis, had told her. "That's when the patient or client is relaxed enough to get into the 'good stuff' but knows time will run out before things are fully explored. It's a kind of self-protection."

CHAPTER 61

The day had been overcast. Janie thought about her many bad relationships with men as she bypassed her mother, who was smoking, and went up to her father's floor. She had been thinking about the bad relationships all the way from Dr. Edberg's office and was beginning to see a pattern.

"I always seem to pick someone who's not available to me. I begin by being wildly in love with him, immediately go to bed with him, and then discover all the things that are wrong with him—or wrong for me. And these are not just subtle flaws or differences. Many times, I learn, if I didn't know or suspect already, that he's married or has children—something I'm not ready for. He may be on a completely different intellectual level, meaning less intelligent than I, and less motivated to learn. Or he may have serious character flaws, such as being an incredible philanderer or user of women, who just wanted to score with me and then move on. Whatever the case, I seem to have this overriding need to take the man away from his current existence—his wife, his kids, his undereducated sensibilities, or his self-indulgent lifestyle."

All this Janie had thought to herself and subsequently told Dr. Edberg.

Being a ray of sunshine as she walked into her father's room felt good but also mildly scary. "When you mean as much to someone as I mean to my daddy, you're always on pins and needles. You want to be perfect, to be everything he wants you to be, and to never let him down," she had told Dr. Edberg.

"And if you let him down?" Dr. Edberg had asked leadingly.

"You just want to die!" Janie had concluded unhesitatingly.

She could tell her father was especially glad to see her as he elevated the bed and extended his arms to hug her.

As Janie leaned over the bed to receive her daddy's still strong bear hug, he did something unusual. He kissed her on the lips.

She started to pull back, with a kind of queasy sensation in the pit of her abdomen. But the daddy bear did not let go and then did something awful—something he had never done before—he forced his tongue into her mouth.

CHAPTER 62

Now at her father's wake, Janie, thirty-six years old and still single, was being the caring social worker for her mother.

She never mentioned the sickening experience of the French kiss to her mother, but she talked it through several times in therapy during the ensuing four years. She never brought it up with her father, nor did he bring it up with her. Janie wanted to believe that he didn't remember it, but she had this horrible feeling at times that he remembered it and that he had enjoyed it.

Janie made sure, from that time on, to never be close to her father if the two of them were alone.

"I guess it's my turn to be vigilant. My mother apparently felt she had to be for years, whether justifiably so or not. She thought my father was very inappropriate with me, and I don't know. I do know that he was very inappropriate with me in the hospital room, back when I was thirty-two," she had told her therapist.

"But you've said you're not sure he knew what he was doing," Dr. Edberg reminded her.

"That's true, but I sure never wanted it to happen again. Maybe I'm protecting Daddy, even after he's gone, when I say he may not have been in his right mind. It's true he'd had a stroke, was medicated, but he seemed so clear and lucid that day about everything else. He lived one or two more fairly good years after that, with the last year or so being hell. He and Mother actually became closer as he became more dependent on her. Surprisingly, they ended their marriage as good companions and sort of seemed to love each other."

"That must make you feel good, knowing and having witnessed their life together ending up well," Dr. Edberg surmised in a supportive way.

"Yes, I guess it does. Really, though, they always said that the first years of their marriage were very close, very loving. Mother had a hard time getting pregnant and was forty-something when I came along. Daddy was almost fifty. I was, I know, a big surprise to them. Sometimes I blame myself for having come into their lives, having been a burden, and having created something of a wedge between them."

"Let's talk about that next time, shall we?" Dr. Edberg asked as he glanced expectantly at the clock on the end table beside Janie.

CHAPTER 63

Against her better judgment, Janie had moved back home. The massive old brick home on a storybook street in Shaker Heights was the essence of success and sophistication back when Janie was a child. She had never appreciated or even known the time and expense that went into keeping an older home functioning and somewhat up-to-date.

Now that her mom was emotionally wandering around the house, unable to keep track of what needed to be done and of what bills needed to be paid, Janie had made the difficult decision to move back home.

"Don't worry, Mother. It will just be long enough for us both to get back on our feet. Daddy's been gone for a while now, and I can help you get organized. The house needs a little work, a face lift inside and out, and I can help you line up some of the people to do the work. Then we can both take turns supervising," she told her mom with a wink and forced cheerfulness.

"I don't want to be a burden, Jane. Your father and I always swore we'd never let you take care of us in our declining years," Elinor said in a voice that reflected sadness and fatigue.

"I'm not taking care of you, Mother. I'm letting you take care of both of us. Once we get the house fixed up, we can sell it and get a condo in Florida, maybe in Boca Raton, where Uncle Ed and Aunt Fran live. We could be right on the water and watch the sun come up every morning."

"But we can't afford it, Jane. You know I'm on a fixed income, and you don't make enough as a social worker to live in that kind of luxury," Elinor said with a sigh.

Thank God, Janie thought. Her mother didn't go into her minilecture about how with her brains, determination, and Uncle Ed's connections at Case Western Reserve's Medical School, Janie really should have been a doctor. "Plus, at medical school, you could have met a nice boy, a doctor, and gotten married. Two doctors, you and your husband, could have made plenty of good money and lived the way you wanted. Instead, you met a bunch of sympathetic marshmallows, social workers, in graduate school, most filled with kindness, but never going to get anywhere financially," Elinor's past words echoed destructively within Janie.

Janie talked fast and jumped in before Elinor could go down that perseverative path. "Mother, I've talked with your banker, and he tells me you have lots of money. He says that Daddy invested well and that your trust will allow you to live very comfortably forever. But he says you're afraid to spend any of it, that you're afraid it will run out."

"I don't know what Sheldon's talking about. He's hardly older than you. I've known him since he was a smart-alecky kid. I just let him be my banker because I promised his mother I would. *Oi, vai!* What does he know?"

"I think he knows enough, Mother." Janie didn't want to give her mother additional information that might confuse her, such as that every time she saw Sheldon, he tried to get friendly and familiar and tell her how unhappily married he was. Janie knew he wanted her to go out with him, but she had sworn off ever knowingly going out with a married man again—even if he took an oath that he was on the verge of consummating his divorce.

"Sheldon is smart, he likes our family, and he wouldn't be a senior trust officer at the bank if he didn't know what he was doing," Janie said resolutely.

"Well, maybe you're right, dear." Elinor sighed again. She loved having Janie worry about her and want to care for her. Deep down, she liked the idea of her daughter moving back home, although with all her heart, she would prefer that she bring with her a little boy or maybe even a little girl. Elinor had trouble relaxing mentally whenever she thought about her likely fate of not having a grandchild.

Elinor lived for years thinking she would never have a child, and then Janie had come along. Elinor had been in her forties, and now, Janie was nearly forty.

Whenever Elinor went to the temple, she only prayed for miracles. The first miracle was that Janie would bring her a grandchild. The second miracle was that she herself would figure out how to help erase the path that her selfish husband Harry had thrust upon Janie through his own sick perversion. And the third miracle the rapidly aging Elinor prayed for was that she could figure out how to tell Janie the truth.

CHAPTER 64

Elinor knew she should tell her daughter the truth. The truth about her life, her father, and her current problems remembering.

She finally found the old Royal typewriter from the back of her closet in the bedroom—converted to an office—and dragged it out. She blew the dust from it, set it on the desk, and checked the ribbon.

"Shit!" she said aloud as she saw the black smudges on her left thumb and index finger. "Well, at least it works," she also said to herself.

Her hands were steady as she inserted the inexpensive typing paper into the Royal's carriage. She sat down, gazed upward, and prepared to type.

But she didn't move. She sat motionless, almost stoic, and then the large tears rolled down her thin-skinned cheeks.

She couldn't bring herself to utter what she suddenly knew—she was no longer able to type.

CHAPTER 65

The following weekend, Janie was not working and had planned to serve a late lunch for the two of them after temple services on Saturday.

"Mother, I have white fish and extra lean corn beef the way you like it. First, though, let's have some matzo-ball soup then a little salad—okay?"

"That's fine, Jane. Thank God for Corky and Lenny's, except for dessert. I made it myself!"

Elinor refrained from adding any critical comments about Janie's cooking. She wanted to stay focused on telling Janie something important today.

"May I prepare a sandwich for you, Mother?" Janie observed her mother's passive nod and continued, "I have something important to tell you. Guess what!"

"Oh, I don't know, honey. What? I want to try to explain something to you today too. Remind me after you tell me your news."

"Actually, it's *our* news, Mother. I purchased, but it's for us, a condo in Boca. You and I can go there during the bad weather up here."

"But how can we afford it?" the increasingly worried, frail Elinor asked. "We haven't sold this house yet—"

"I can afford it—I bought it for us. I used some of the money from my retirement account at the counseling center, and now that I have four weeks of vacation, I can fly back and forth from here to Florida during the winter months, maybe working three days a week."

"But, Jane, what will I do if you're not there? I don't know my way around, I'm scared to drive, and I'll be all alone . . ." Her voice trailed off in its well-developed, guilt-invoking tone.

"Mother! Uncle Ed and Aunt Fran will be neighbors. They are only one building away—you can walk there any time you want."

"Oh, I forgot. I forgot they are moving to Florida. They're going to Boca something."

"Boca *Raton*, Mother. They moved there five years ago." Janie was doing her best to be patient. She knew her mom was developing dementia or something. Sometimes, though, she seemed to forget selectively as a way of increasing her emotional dependency and passive power.

"Yes, I knew that. I just forgot. When you get to be my age, it's hard to remember things, even things that happened yesterday. But I can remember stuff that happened years ago, back when your father was alive, very clearly. What's that called, Jane?"

"Maybe it's just part of getting older, Mother. It doesn't have to have a name or a diagnosis."

"Diagnosis . . . that reminds me . . ." Elinor obviously was exerting effort to get her brain working.

"What, Mother?" Janie, on the surface, appeared to be concerned.

"I have something important to tell you, Jane. Boca sounds good, good for you, but I don't know about for me." After a long pause, Elinor continued. "I think you're aware, honey, that I'm losing my memory."

"Oh, Mother—" Janie tried to intercede and break the flow of this discourse. She suspected what she didn't want to hear.

"Wait—listen, Jane." Her mother desperately wanted to pass on important information to her. She had thought for years about how to tell Janie but, until just recently, had never figured out a way to do so.

"Please try to understand, honey. I need to tell you some details before I forget. And once I forget something, it may never come back to me. Last week, I sat down to type you a letter. I ended up hurt and paralyzed. I couldn't do a thing—I forgot how to type!"

"Mother, don't worry . . . I love you, and I will take care of you." Janie reached over and hugged her, starting to cry herself.

"But I was able to do what I wanted to do. I was able to write you a letter. It was a long letter and hard to write. It took me two or three days to get it done. I had to write it, not type it, but I was able to remember everything I wanted to tell you."

"What do you mean, Mother? Just tell me what you want to tell me. You don't have to write me a letter." Janie was puzzled and was beginning to think her mom was being somewhat silly.

"Jane, I have Alzheimer's. Dr. Feldman confirmed it a month ago. Physically, I'm in pretty good shape and may live a long time. My body is probably going to outlive my mind though. Dr. Feldman is giving me huge doses of selenium and natural brain stimulants as well as some experimental drugs he has his cousin bring in from Canada."

Now Janie was crying without restraint. "Mother, don't tell me all this. None of us knows how long we're going to live or how long we're going to stay lucid. I wish you listened as much to Sheldon Ksonska, your banker, as you do to Dr. Feldman!"

"Please, Jane, I mean Janie. Let me finish. What I'm trying to tell you is that I spent a few days writing you a letter, telling you things I've wanted to tell you or tried to tell you for years. I needed to write the letter while I'm still lucid as you would say. I put it in your father's and my safety deposit box and instructed Sheldon, who's not been a bad trust officer, to keep our keys to the box and to give them to you when I die—or when Alzheimer's takes over."

"You mean you don't want to be aware of what's going on when I read your letter?" Janie thought the whole thing sounded strange, maybe even ominous.

This was probably some kind of bad news. Her mother had tried to share bad news with her in the past, but Janie had to admit it had not worked out well, partly because her mother had told her things about her past that Janie couldn't remember or couldn't verify.

The business about her father molesting her was hard to imagine and had never really come to light in all the years of therapy with Dr. Edberg. He had even tried to hypnotize her a few times. Thank God, he had finally retired. Janie no longer had to go and see him weekly, more out of obligation than as a result of perceived benefit.

Maybe her mother had imagined the things about her dad—she knew her mother wouldn't out-and-out lie about it. Maybe she had gotten carried away in her imagination because she wanted the close relationship her husband suddenly developed with their new daughter for herself.

Paranoia can be a strange thing, very hard to explain, particularly its origins. Janie knew this from her schooling and clinical work. One thing she felt certain about, though, she knew her mother was developing Alzheimer's.

CHAPTER 66

"I will read the letter whenever you want, or I won't read it until you're gone. I promise." Janie wanted to reassure her mother. She was being sincere.

Besides, if it was more bad news about the past, why worry about it? "There's nothing a person can do about the past. It was what it was." She remembered in a flash, having once said the same thing to Dr. Edberg.

"That's partially true," the ever so slightly directive therapist had responded. "What's important is how we interpret that past and what use we make of it for the present and for the future."

So far, she had made little, if any, use of the notion that her father had molested her. How could she use that even if it were true? It was hidden beneath too many layers of experience, time, and repression. Maybe it was a part of her past that should remain hidden.

"Now, Mother, I want you to promise me something. I promised you I wouldn't read the letter yet. Will you promise me something?"

"I guess, Janie . . . what is it?" Elinor had an ever so slight sparkle in one of her no-longer tearing eyes. She seemed pleased that she and her daughter were so engaged and had become so close in the last few years. She was pleased that she could please her daughter by conscientiously calling her Janie.

"Mother, promise me that you—you and I together—will live every day to the fullest, that we'll try to be positive and optimistic, that we'll make the most out of every adventure, every trip to Boca."

"Okay . . . I promise I will try."

"You've got to try, Mother. That way, we can have fun, we can laugh, and we can live a good life together. I do love you, you know."

"I love you too, Janie. I will live every day as if it is my last. You know, I think I heard someone say that once."

From that time on, when Elinor called her daughter by name, she only called her Janie.

Chapter 67

Janie and Elinor had fun together in Florida. The condo Janie bought was on the ocean, close to an inland waterway that went back to a bay surrounded by huge homes. Each one seemed more lavish than the one just viewed. It appeared that owners wanted to be envied but unseen as paths from docks to the homes were crowded by foliage.

The homes, except for the rooftops, were essentially hidden from the curious boaters who trolled for a glimpse of who lived just outside of view.

"Why does the water down there always look so choppy?" Elinor asked Janie more than once as she looked from their windows down to the Atlantic shoreline below.

"As I've said, Mother, I'm not sure, but I think it's because it's so close to the opening that goes back into the bay. Maybe there's some kind of suction, or at least there's a ripple effect from all the boats that come and go along the channel. Do you like it?"

"Like what?" Elinor's attention had already been diverted.

"The water, Ma, the choppy water down there."

"Yes, I like it. I like it very much. I never thought I could leave the house we lived in for years. But we're happy here, aren't we, Janie?"

"Yes, we are, Mother," the supportive daughter said as she hugged the thin, unsteady woman whose aging process was in high gear.

"Mother, have you lost more weight? What am I going to do with you? I'm going to have to take better care of you and make sure you remember to eat," Janie said with a forced smile that covered her accumulated worry.

It was becoming harder and harder to go back to Cleveland and try to be an effective therapist because her mother's Alzheimer's was steadily progressing. She was forgetting to eat, forgetting to brush her teeth, and occasionally forgetting where she was.

Uncle Ed and Aunt Fran were not able to keep tabs on Elinor much longer. What she really needed was constant care.

"Why don't you put your mom in a retirement home that specializes in caring for Alzheimer's patients?" Aunt Fran had asked.

"I know it may come to that, Aunt Fran, but I want to keep her with me as long as I can. I may have to give up my practice in Cleveland, but that's not all bad. I'm thinking I can have someone stay with her during the day while I develop my business down here. You know I'm licensed now in Florida too, don't you?"

"Yes, and we're very proud of you, Janie. Your uncle and I are here to help you, you know that. We will be glad to pay for a sitter or nurse or whatever they're called until you get established here.

"I wouldn't think it would take very long to get your practice up and running here. I told Ed just last week that everybody in Boca needs to slow down and smell the roses. It seems like the older they are, the bigger the hurry they're in. And they don't waste any time on politeness. I guess that makes sense though. They feel they don't have much time left. Most of them need some help, some therapy or something, to figure out how to slow down, enjoy what they have, and appreciate the people around them.

You'll be glad to know I have a visiting nurse coming to meet Mother tomorrow. She's going to spend the weekend with us, and hopefully, she and Mother will hit it off."

"That's great, Janie," said Fran.

"I interviewed a number of people, but when I talked with Estelle, that's her name, I really thought she was the best. An interesting thing about her though . . ."

"What's that?" asked Fran.

"She looks like me. I don't know if it will be good or bad. Mom may not be able to tell who's who—whether it's me or Estelle."

"Oh, I don't believe that, sweetie."

"Why not?" Janie asked.

"Because a mother never forgets her own daughter."

CHAPTER 68

Elinor and Estelle immediately hit it off well. "Why, you look just like my daughter. Is that why you're hiring this beautiful young woman, Janie?"

"Not really, Mother. Estelle was definitely the best qualified, most impressive nurse I interviewed. She lives fairly close, in Hollywood, and has excellent experience helping people like you and me," Janie responded.

"Are you Jewish, honey?" Elinor sensed that she was but wanted to have it confirmed.

"No, Mrs. Rosen. I am not. I am Hispanic. My parents were born in Cuba," the confident and proud senorita responded.

Janie felt good, felt positive, that her mother's rather brash questioning had not thrown the twenty-something young woman for a loop. Janie squinted and looked closely at Estelle and felt flattered. She saw a beautifully smooth, naturally tanned skin; a thin, muscular body; and a very youthful face surrounded by dark, curly hair.

Janie wished she looked as good as Estelle or at least felt as good about herself as Estelle seemed to feel.

"Are you sure about that, young princess?" Elinor continued her direct, less than tactful questioning of Estelle.

"I beg your pardon, ma'am?" Estelle responded.

"Are you sure your parents are both from Cuba? I think one of your parents was Jewish. Do you think maybe you were adopted?"

"Mother!" Janie intervened, staring critically at her puzzled mother. "Estelle knows who she is, and it's rude to ask those kinds of questions. You're going to cause her to quit before she even gets started—"

"It's all right, Ms. Rosen. I understand. There's no problem . . . Mrs. Rosen, would you like for me to start coming to visit you every day?"

"Absolutely," Elinor responded, somewhat confused but not particularly concerned about why her daughter had seemed so upset. "In fact, Janie said if I like you, you can spend the weekend. And I really like you."

CHAPTER 69

Janie had put off the inevitable long enough. Her counseling and therapy business was doing well, and Estelle and her mother were doing extremely well together. It was time to go to Cleveland and close her practice there.

"Hello?" Aunt Fran answered her cell phone after a few rings, probably having looked at the caller ID to make sure it was someone with whom she wanted to talk.

"Aunt Fran, it's Janie."

"Janie, how are you? How's your mother?"

"I'm fine, she's fine, and we're doing great. I swear, I think Estelle has been a God-send. Mother has not complained, has not been depressed, and has not gone downhill memory-wise since Estelle's been with us."

"That's wonderful, child. It truly is. I'm so glad everyone's doing so well. And is Estelle doing okay?"

"Yes, she and Mom have really bonded. As you know, they run around together to yard sales, to auctions, and last week when I was working late, they even went to the dog races in Hollywood."

"Oh my god, Janie . . . Do you think that's a good idea? Is it safe? What was Estelle thinking?"

"I'm sure she thought it was safe, and her whole strategy seems to be to keep Mother busy and on her toes. She constantly asks Mother questions, like a parent would ask a nine-year-old. 'If our tickets cost $5 each and I give the nice lady $20, how much change will I get back?' She's trying to keep Mother involved doing crossword puzzles and word searches. It's pretty amazing—Mother really hasn't regressed."

"Maybe Estelle is trying to be a therapist like you, honey," Aunt Fran volunteered.

"Maybe she is . . . She certainly has a lot of patience for the job. I'm headed up to Cleveland this weekend and wanted to make sure you and Uncle Ed are going to be home in case Estelle needs you for something."

"Of course, dear, we'll be here," Aunt Fran answered supportively. "I'm glad you're going to get away for a little while—you need some time for yourself."

"What do you mean?" Janie felt herself tensing up.

"I mean it's time you devote more attention to building your own life, your future. You need a man to share your life with, honey. You know, someone you can marry. You're spending all this valuable time taking care of your mother."

"I know, I know, Aunt Fran." Janie heard an edge in her own voice. "Right now, Mother needs me—I'm all she has . . ."

"That may be true, Janie, but you need to find a man and get married. You're not getting any younger, you know, and it would be so special to bring a grandchild home to your mother."

Aunt Fran's words lingered with Janie as she flew to Cleveland. She knew her aunt was right, that she really should get married. She had never gone into much detail with her aunt or anyone other than Dr. Edberg for that matter, about how hard she had tried to get married. She knew that she had scared off some of the men because of her not-so-invisible desperation.

And the older she became, the more difficult it was to meet decent men who offered some promise and a willingness to commit. It wasn't as if one or two really good men had gotten away—she couldn't really say she had ever been involved with a really good man. *Maybe I just always set my sights too low; maybe I feel at some level that I don't deserve a truly good man,* she thought.

The trip was mostly uneventful. Janie tried to get together with some of her old buddies from high school and college, but no one was available. The ones she reached by phone said they wanted to take a rain check and, next time, give them more lead time.

She had an appointment Saturday morning at the Beachwood branch of her bank with Sheldon Ksonska.

"Do you think your mother would mind if I came to see her?" Sheldon asked early on in the meeting after having embraced Janie firmly and having tried unsuccessfully to kiss her on the lips.

"I don't know, but why would you want to do that?" Janie asked, noticing that Sheldon had lost a fair amount of weight, was wearing an expensive suit, but was not wearing a wedding band.

"Well, she and your father, now your mother and you, have one of the larger trusts for our bank to manage. We have a few branches in Florida, and I could come visit them and look in on your mother. You know, see if she has any questions or anything that she wants me to do."

"I guess that's fine," Janie answered, presuming that Sheldon was probably angling to get some time alone with her and maybe finally get her into bed while in Florida.

"Very good. I will set something up and coordinate with you, Janie." Sheldon beamed, showing his beautifully veneered teeth and winning smile. He looked very handsome and seemed to be more poised than she remembered him as being.

Janie learned in her meeting with Sheldon that she and her mother were prospering. Sheldon and the bank had managed their assets well, and her mother had consistently refused to touch any income or interest from the estate. Janie would like to alter her mother's frugal approach, but it would be very difficult to do as long as her mother was thinking clearly enough to know what was going on. By the time her mother would get to enjoy her wealth, she would be in no mental state to appreciate the joy.

Janie guessed she would continue working to support both of them for now, also utilizing her mother's social security and income from a small stock portfolio she also had refused to sell.

If and when the Alzheimer's overcame her mother, Janie would use her power of attorney to set up routine distributions of the interest generated by her mother's estate.

And if her mother became that impaired, maybe then she would be able to find out what was in the letter.

CHAPTER 70

"What have you busy little bees been doing while I was gone?" Janie asked her mother and Estelle upon her return from Cleveland. "It looks like you've taken up a new hobby—sewing."

"Oh, honey, you won't believe it! Estelle has taught me how to make tiny stitches to piece together patterns for a quilt." Elinor held up a large square of multicolored patchwork as proudly as if she were Betsy Ross.

"That's beautiful, Mother, it really is. Where did you learn to do all this, Estelle?"

"My family, for generations, has known how to sew and how to make do with next to nothing. My mother tells stories of looking through trash piles to find rags to use for quilts."

"Well, I'm impressed. Did the two of you have any problems while I was gone?" Janie thought she knew the answer.

"Not at all," they answered in unison.

"Mother, I saw Sheldon Ksonska while I was in Cleveland, and he tells me we're rich. He says we should start spending some of the money you and Daddy worked so hard to save." Janie hesitated, thinking maybe she should not have said this in front of Estelle; but then, she trusted Estelle nearly completely.

"Did he try to seduce you?" Elinor startled Janie by asking.

"Mother! What's wrong with you—why do you ask that?"

"Oh, I know a lot more than you give me credit for," Elinor responded, smiling in a way that a wise person might.

"That's right, Janie. Your mom, my buddy El, is sharp as a tack and getting sharper—aren't you?" Estelle hugged Elinor and prepared to leave.

Janie didn't like the nickname "El" that Estelle had started calling her mother, but Elinor seemed to like it. It just seemed to Janie that Estelle was trying a little too hard to butter up her mother.

To her credit, though, Estelle always seemed to know when it was best to take off. She clearly was sensing that the conversation about Sheldon Ksonska was one that Janie preferred to have with her mother alone, without Estelle present.

"So I'll see both of you on Wednesday?" Estelle asked, reconfirming that she was going to be off duty on Monday and Tuesday.

"Yes," both Janie and Elinor responded as Estelle moved with catlike grace toward the door.

"Be careful," Janie advised as her youthful look-alike opened and shut the door behind her.

"What's this about Sheldon?" Janie asked Elinor immediately.

"Honey, I just know a lot of things—probably more than you give me credit for. Estelle says I know more than I even give myself credit for knowing, especially now that I have Alzheimer's."

"I'm sure that's true," Janie responded reassuringly and lovingly.

"I've never told you before, but I knew since Sheldon was a neighborhood smart aleck that he had a crush on you. I don't think you ever felt the same about him, though, did you?"

"Not really, Mother, but I didn't know he had a crush on me," Janie responded with some bewilderment. She almost said, "had the hots for me" instead of "had a crush on me," but she decided to repeat the words her mother had used.

"If I had known that, I might have gone out with him at the time," Janie continued.

"Hmm—then he would have been my son-in-law. Maybe that would have been good for all of us. He wouldn't have ended up with that pale, wispy gentile girl from Cleveland Heights whose family had all that money."

"Mother, I probably wouldn't have ended up marrying him."

"You never know . . ."

"Besides, he should have told me he liked me and should have asked me out."

"He was probably afraid you would reject him. You were the prettiest girl in Beachwood, you know."

"Mother, you always say that, but you're biased. Besides, he waited until he married that Mary Ellen, or whatever his wife's name is, before he showed any interest in me."

"I know that, even though you never told me. That's why I didn't want him to be my trust officer at first. I thought he should have asked you out a long time ago when the two of you were in high school or college. And I didn't approve of the way he started trying to get you to go out with him after he was married until he explained it."

"Mother, explained what? What and when did Sheldon talk with you about me?" Janie was somewhat irritated, but somewhat flattered.

"You know, I saw him from time to time at the bank before we moved down here, and he always asked about you. I told him he missed the boat by not marrying a nice Jewish girl like you. Then he made kind of a confession." Elinor's eyes looked toward the ceiling.

"What?" Now Janie felt a strong sense of suddenly being attracted to Sheldon. Maybe she should have recognized that he wanted to ask her out way back then. But now he was married . . . although maybe not.

"Mother, what was his confession?"

"He said he was always in love with you but was too shy or insecure to ask you out until after he was married. I guess once he got married, even if you turned him down, he still had his wife to fall back on. And according to him, you always rejected the advances he made after he got married. You did, didn't you, honey?"

CHAPTER 71

Janie answered her mother honestly but not completely. She truthfully told Elinor that she had never gone to bed with Sheldon, although he had tried. She didn't go into detail about some of their passionate trysts in her car or in his office.

Two weeks later, Janie answered the phone excitedly when the caller ID indicated a call from the Cleveland bank's trust department.

"Janie, how are you?" Sheldon's smooth, comfortable voice on the other end of the line asked.

"I'm fine, Sheldon. Are you coming to Florida? To Boca?" Janie blushed and winced, thinking that her voice conveyed more excitement than she wanted Sheldon to sense from her.

"Yes, I am. This Friday, in fact. Can you and your mother be available?"

"Yes, I can make myself available, and Mother's always available."

"Good. May I pick you up and take the two of you to lunch?"

"Sure," Janie responded warmly. How long will you be in Florida?"

"For part of the weekend. I also want to see your aunt and uncle while I'm there, probably for lunch on Saturday." Sheldon paused, and continued abruptly, "Janie, I wanted to tell you when you were here last month—Mary Ellen and I are getting a divorce."

"Oh my—I'm sorry. I mean, I'm sorry if you're sorry." Even though she was a therapist, Janie felt uncertain about what to say.

"Thanks, Janie. Actually, I'm not sorry, I'm happy. I made a mistake a long time ago getting married to Mary Ellen. We had dated for a long time. I liked it that her family was rich, and getting married to her seemed like a safe thing to do."

"It's interesting how things work out, isn't it?" Janie mused. "Maybe she was a pretty good choice at the time but doesn't seem like a good choice today."

"I don't really know, but I doubt it. I guess I had no idea she would eventually want to be the boss in the relationship. When she said 'jump,' she expected me to ask 'how high?'"

Sheldon's voice became deeper and very serious. "I think I should have tried to go with you and see if you and I could become a couple."

"Oh boy . . . thanks, Sheldon. Maybe we can talk about this on Friday when you're here. Can we go out that night, just the two of us?" Janie was surprised by Sheldon's directness and, in turn, her own.

"I'd love to have dinner with you, Janie, but I don't want to talk about Mary Ellen or what went wrong in the marriage."

"We can find lots of things to talk about," Janie replied, wondering if maybe his wife had found out Sheldon had the hots for her. Janie didn't feel guilty.

"I just want us to start fresh and really get to know each other. Two people, both who grew up in Cleveland, went different directions and are now getting acquainted. I don't want our histories apart or our history together to get in the way. I don't want to analyze the past and talk about my marriage or any significant relationships you've had. And the last thing I want to talk about is why you and I had those passionate moments when I tried to make love to you."

"Okay, okay." Janie gulped quietly. "That sounds like a good plan. We're friends, we're starting out fresh, and we'll get to know each other without a lot of encumbrances."

Janie had feelings of exhilaration as if she had climbed to the top of a mountain and could see a long way in all directions when she hung up the phone.

Friday seemed so far away.

CHAPTER 72

Lunch at Houston's, which had quickly become Janie's favorite restaurant, had all the right ingredients—cordiality, lightheartedness, sincerity, and occasional serious conversation.

"You two look so beautiful together," Elinor said admiringly from her lone side of the rich, tufted leather booth in Houston's.

"Oh, Mother! You're always so complimentary and so biased. I do think that you look very handsome, Sheldon." Janie had been watching Sheldon since she had gone down to the lobby of their high-rise condominium building to meet him. He looked very sharp, somewhat like a banker on holiday, with his blue-and-white wide pinstriped shirt, tan gabardine slacks, and blue blazer. Still no wedding band, she noticed.

"Thanks, Janie. You always look great, look beautiful. You haven't changed since college—the therapy business must be agreeing with you."

"Sheldon, you're getting as bad as Mother. I know you mean what you say, but you're looking at me through rose-colored glasses."

"Not really . . . how is the therapy going? Have you got a good practice going down here?"

"Yes, I guess so. I'm happy with it. I have great clients." Janie could tell Sheldon was genuinely interested.

"How do you define *good* clients?" Sheldon asked with a chuckle.

"Clients who are reliable—they always show up, and they always pay their bills."

The three of them laughed at the same time, and Janie continued, "Seriously, I have built up a strong base of referring professionals who send me an interesting mix—young, old, male, and female."

"I really admire and respect what you do," Sheldon said as Elinor nodded energetically.

"And she's extremely capable at it too." The proud mother punctuated her nodding.

"Well, maybe I can get her to work on you." Sheldon looked squarely at Elinor.

"What do you mean, Sheldon?" Elinor asked, somewhat surprised.

"I want her to give you some counseling, some supportive words that will encourage you to start spending that mountain of money you've left up in Cleveland at the bank."

"Janie's told me over and over that I need to start spending some of the cash from our investments, but I've been hardheaded," Elinor admitted.

"Mother, you're not hardheaded, just conservative," Janie offered supportively.

"I love you, Janie. You look so beautiful, so radiant today with Sheldon. I'm going to follow your advice."

"What—" Janie reacted.

"I'm going to start spending our money, pay off the condo, and do whatever you and Sheldon tell me to do."

"Mother, that's wonderful! We'll enjoy the money, every penny you've saved. All the money you and Daddy built up."

"Oh, that reminds me, Janie. One more thing—" Elinor was now squinting, wrinkling her face.

"What?" Sheldon asked this time, sensing that Janie was almost afraid to ask.

"I want Janie to open the letter I left for her on one condition."

"What's that, Mother? What's the condition?" Janie had an uneasy feeling.

"I want Sheldon to be there when you open it, to be your support. Maybe even your therapist if you need one."

"That's fine with me," Janie responded. "Sheldon, how do you feel about it?" Janie looked into Sheldon's attentive eyes with high expectations.

"Sure, that's fine," he said, somewhat enthusiastically. "How about if you fly back to Cleveland with me tomorrow, Janie?"

Chapter 73

When Janie said yes to Sheldon's suggestion, she didn't realize that arrangements would be so easy. The bank's corporate jet was waiting at the Boca Raton Executive Airport to take Sheldon back to Cleveland Saturday afternoon after his luncheon with Aunt Fran and Uncle Ed.

All Janie needed to do was pack for a couple of overnights, and the bank's jet would bring her back Monday afternoon.

The plane ride north was smooth and uneventful, with only the two pilots, Janie, and Sheldon on board.

Janie and Sheldon talked about college, things they should have done differently in college, and what they wanted to achieve in their lives. Not surprisingly to either, both of them wanted to help people, to make a significant difference in the way people succeeded in life.

During dinner Saturday night at Noggin's in Warrensville Heights, Sheldon said how pleased he was that Elinor had decided to start enjoying her wealth.

"You're right, and I was afraid she'd never get to enjoy it," Janie agreed. "Thank goodness, she listened to you, Sheldon." She reached across the table and held her hand on his hand.

"What do you think is in the letter, Janie?" Sheldon asked without forewarning.

"Oh gosh, I don't know. I figure it's something bad, something about my childhood. She told me once that she caught my dad touching me or something when I was very young. I don't remember it, though, thank God, and I think I have chosen to believe that she imagined it, that it didn't really happen."

"What difference does it make now, especially since you don't remember it?" Sheldon was now using both his hands to hold her hands.

"I don't really know. Maybe it doesn't matter now. Whatever happened, happened. I spent quite a bit of time in therapy myself, trying to see if maybe I was damaged in some way as a result of early childhood trauma."

"If you're damaged, then everyone should be. You're one of the most stable, feet-on-the-ground kinds of person I've ever known," Sheldon said admiringly.

"Whatever is in the letter, I'm glad you'll be there with me, Sheldon. I really am."

"So am I, honey," Sheldon said before kissing her hand.

CHAPTER 74

Monday morning, Sheldon helped Janie open the large safety deposit box with the bank key and the customer key Elinor had entrusted to him a few years earlier.

Because of his station in the bank, Sheldon was able to bring the lock box into his large corner office.

"Are you nervous, sweetie?" Sheldon asked as he sat the box directly onto his leather-topped desk. It was the same desk where he had once passionately kissed Janie and had taken her bra off before she finally stopped him. She tried not to remember it at first but then enjoyed the memory.

"Yes and no, actually. I'm more nervous about Mother right now, and I'm getting ahead of myself. I'm thinking more about getting back to Boca this afternoon to check up on her."

"Why? Isn't she okay when you're gone?" Sheldon mirrored Janie's concern.

"Ordinarily, yes, but last night she sounded terrible, not like herself. Estelle, the nurse, said Mother had been wandering around the condo all day, calling for me, saying she knew I would never come back. I think she was worried about how I might react to the letter."

"Did you actually talk to your mother or just to the nurse?" Now Sheldon was worried.

"Yeah, I talked with Mother, but she was, like I said, not herself. She seemed confused and kept asking why I was on the phone and why didn't I just come home. I tried to tell her I'd be home in a few hours, about seventeen hours, but all of a sudden, there was silence. Then Estelle came on the line and said Mother was in bed and wanted to sleep and did not want to talk on the phone. Estelle said she had given Mother some sleeping medication, which ticked me off at her a little bit."

"I'm sure Estelle was just doing what she thought was best," Sheldon said, trying to reassure.

"Maybe, but I hope you don't mind. As soon as we read the letter, I need to go to the airport," Janie said.

"No problem. Did you talk to your mother this morning?"

"Yeah, but she sounded kind of out of it. Morose, sort of. I wanted to talk to Estelle, but apparently, she was picking up breakfast for the two of them at Flakowitz Bagels.

"Don't worry, I'm sure your mother's just missing her precious daughter. I'll drive you to the airport in a few minutes. The plane will be waiting, and you may be home in time to take her back to Houston's for lunch. I want you to call me as soon as you get home and see your mother."

"I will—you're beautifully supportive, Sheldon." She stretched upward and kissed him on the lips—nothing heavy, nothing seductive, and nothing secretive or forbidden. She was beginning to love Sheldon, and felt that with him there, she could handle whatever was in the letter.

Together, they opened the envelope and quietly read Elinor's once-meticulous handwriting.

Janie:

> *Please know above everything, I love you. I made mistakes in my life, but you were never a mistake. I never wanted you to think that you might be a mistake or loved only partially.*
>
> *Your father and I loved you from the moment we saw you and knew that you were special and that you were ours. I never wanted to tell you, and he agreed that you were biologically created by two other people but just for us.*
>
> *An attorney named Simon Federer arranged for us to meet you and adopt you when you were only five days old. You were a miracle and a gift from heaven. Mr. Federer told us you were born Jewish, and we knew you would make our family complete.*
>
> *I never wanted to tell you, but your father threatened to hurt you and me by telling. I told you he touched you, but I don't know if that's true or not. I saw him touching himself*

in your room, but you were not there. He threatened me, and I threatened him. A terrible way to live and I tried to protect you. I hope you can understand and forgive me. Maybe he was innocent. He said so before he died.

Always remember that I love you. I always wanted you and never regretted having you. You have always been my world.

Love,
Mother

Janie was in shock all the way to the airport. She knew Sheldon was there for comfort and support, but she didn't feel she needed it. She was glad the father she had known and adored had never molested her. The kiss later on in the hospital had been inappropriate, but he must not have known what he was doing because of the strokes.

Being adopted didn't really feel all that bad to her, although it might feel worse later. The only two parents she had ever known were the two who had raised her. Each of them had a few hang-ups or issues, so at least now she didn't need to worry about those being passed on to her genetically.

"At least my worst fears about my daddy were not true," she said, suddenly breaking the silence and Sheldon's intent stare at the icy road ahead.

"That's good, that's good," Sheldon replied, not knowing what else to say.

"Have you gotten a hold of your mother?" he asked, shifting subjects, bringing things back to the present in almost a mechanical kind of way.

Janie shook her head. "I've tried the condo, Estelle's cell phone, and there's no answer. I can't wait to get home."

"I know Elinor will be as relieved as you to have you home."

"I know . . . I want to tell her I understand why she did what she did, you know, not tell me."

"That's good. She'll be relieved to hear that. You can tell from the letter she feels guilty," Sheldon said as he put his right hand firmly on Janie's left leg, just above the knee.

"I just don't want her to be anxious or worried or to regress because of some deep, dark secret she's carried with her for thirty-nine years."

"Thirty-eight, I believe—thirty-nine next month," Sheldon remarked, having committed her birthday to memory a long time ago.

He kissed her fully at the hangar, and his body felt wonderful, firmly against hers. "Come back and see me," he said and smiled a loving smile that stayed with her for a long time on the flight.

She rushed home from the Boca Raton airport, still unable to reach her mother.

As she got off the elevator onto their floor, she suddenly felt panicky. She knew something was wrong by the sight of the door to their condo ajar.

She burst into the condo, ran through the foyer past the kitchen and dining area to the large family room. The sliding glass doors to the balcony were wide open, and the chilly, damp wind was whipping the curtains back into the room.

Janie ran onto the unprotected balcony, absorbed the scene of the turbulent Atlantic expanse with fear, and instinctively looked down at the beach below. Thank God no one was there.

She then heard a whimpering behind her and wheeled around to see her mother, old, tired, and crumpled on the floor, leaning against the base of the couch.

"Mother! My god, what's wrong?"

"Why, nothing's wrong. I'm just waiting for my daughter to come back."

"That's me, Mother—it's me, Janie. I'm your daughter."

"Oh, that's good. I thought when you left and took all the stuff with you to Flakowitz that you might not come back."

"That wasn't me, it was Estelle. What stuff? Where?" Janie scanned the room and quickly recognized that two valuable paintings and all the glassware in the hutch had disappeared.

She knew without looking that jewelry, money, and other items would be gone.

Estelle always knew when it was best to take off.

PART V

CHAPTER 75

Kenny's death was a harsh blow to Angela. He had been the most significant influence in her life, yet even though she loved him, she had a great deal of ambivalence about the relationship. Before her one-night stand with Fredrik, she had determined she needed to leave Kenny and get out on her own.

After the difficult night with Fredrik, she determined she needed to stay with Kenny, perhaps get couples counseling and try to build a healthy, mutually satisfying relationship. Maybe she had fantasized they would get married someday.

One thing Angela knew for certain: she had to get out of the sex-for-hire business, although Kenny had a nicer way of describing it. Before his death, she had worried that Kenny would never let her quit generating money that way. For one thing, he needed the money for his gambling appetite—or as Red would call it, gambling addiction.

"I came as soon as I heard the news, baby," the tall silver-haired gentleman told the obviously grieving, unsteady young girl.

"Oh, Red, that's so wonderful of you. Thank you," Angela said as she accepted his affirming embrace.

"What can I do?" the compassionate car dealer asked.

"Nothing, really. I'm glad you're here. I hope you will come to the funeral . . ."

"You know I will, honey." His eyes looked lovingly at the most beautiful lady he had ever known. It seemed like years ago that they had actually played together sexually, and he was hoping that they could eventually resume their intimacies. Out of respect, if nothing else, Red had already decided to wait a couple of weeks after Kenny was buried to try to ease back into his relationship with Angela.

"Red, I need you to do me a favor," Angela said, and he didn't exactly like her tone and look.

"Sure, honey. What is it?"

"I want you to come to the funeral as Kenny's friend or mentor or whatever—not as my former sex partner."

"That's fine. No problem." Although his words did not reflect the sting he felt from Angela's words. Red saw himself as much more than a "sex partner" but rather as an older lover who had Angela's best interests at heart.

"Two things I want to tell you, and we don't need to ever talk about them again, okay?" Red continued.

"Oh yes, Red. And I'm sorry." Angela sensed she had hurt his feelings. "You're more than a former sex partner. You were and are a good friend."

That made Red feel a little better, but he didn't see any doorway into the bedroom with Angela opening back up. "The Werner guy forgave all of Kenny's debts, so there's not going to be any claim against his assets. Obviously, you did a great job with his son."

"Oh thanks, I guess . . ." Angela hardly knew how to respond. She appreciated Kenny's huge debt being paid off or forgiven, but she didn't like the sound of being told she'd done a great job having sex all night with an unappealing person.

"And the second thing, I've paid for Kenny's funeral and was able to pay off yours and Kenny's condo. You own it now, free and clear. This way, you won't have to disrupt your life, your school, or anything else. If you want me to help you work up a budget, I can do that, and I will fill in any financial gaps along the way. It's real important that you get a college degree—take it from me—I never got mine."

"Red, you've always been so good to me," Angela said as she embraced him again. She appreciated and would accept what he had done for her, but after the funeral, she would tell him that she didn't want any more of his financial help. She did not want to continue her dependency on Red or on any man.

Kenny had helped her learn that lesson without really trying to teach it.

CHAPTER 76

"Mrs. Angela Chessin?"

"No, sir. This is Angela Capelli. May I help you?" Angela responded to the six-thirty-in-the-evening call from the National Way Insurance Corporation.

"Oh, I'm sorry. I'm looking for Mr. Kenny Chessin's widow. Excuse me, I'm Victor Ross from National Ways. Mr. Chessin named Angela Capelli Chessin as one of his beneficiaries in a life insurance policy he held with us."

"Kenny and I lived together. Maybe he thought I was his wife by common law marriage. Maybe I was—I don't know anything about those laws in Ohio."

"Well, forgive me. Ms. Capelli then. I wonder if I could come by and see you tomorrow. Will you be at home?" the smooth-voiced Victor Ross asked.

"I will be home in the morning until ten thirty when I have to leave for class. How would that be?" Angela asked the stranger.

"Perfect. This won't take long. I will be there at nine o'clock if that's all right."

"That's fine," Angela said, wanting to be accommodating. "Do you need directions how to get here?"

"Oh no, I've driven by your place a couple of times," Victor answered. "One more thing, Ms. Capelli—"

"What?"

"We're sorry for your loss."

Angela hung up the phone and concluded she didn't like this man. He was a little too friendly and seemed to be hiding something. Why had he called her Mrs. Chessin, and why had he driven by her condo twice?

She needed to see him face-to-face and try to figure out if he was on the up and up. She knew Kenny had a life insurance policy, but she didn't know for what amount. And this guy Ross said she was one of the beneficiaries—plural. So who else was a beneficiary?

CHAPTER 77

The next morning, Victor Ross rang the doorbell at nine thirty and apologized profusely for being late. "I was at another dear woman's home, an older lady, and I stayed longer than I had planned, trying to comfort her."

Before her, Angela saw a thin man of slight stature, bespectacled, conservatively dressed in a worn gray suit, white shirt, and nondescript tie. "Don't worry about it. As long as I leave at ten thirty for class, I'll be fine."

Against her better judgment, she found herself sort of liking this little man, almost feeling sorry for him.

"May I come in for a few minutes?" Victor asked politely, handing her a business card from National Ways, complete with logo, address, and title.

"Why, Mr. Ross, I see you're a regional vice president of claims, all the way from Washington DC. What are you doing way out here in little ole Columbus?" Angela asked.

"Well, I had several calls to make, people to see during their grief. We truly are sorry, Ms. Capelli, for your loss and hope that we can provide you with financial comfort and relief. How are you holding up?"

Angela's wariness began to rise again. Why was he acting so polite and nice, almost like a minister making his rounds? He seemed to be beating around the bush instead of getting to the point, which he had said yesterday would only take a few minutes. And why would a person who seemed very meticulous, detailed, and orderly be thirty minutes late and not even call?

"Thank you, Mr. Ross. I appreciate your concern. What do you need from me?"

"I have a few questions to ask you and paperwork to sign, of course, but my company and I want to be able to help you out in any way that you need. You know, financially. For example, if you have funeral expenses to pay, a mortgage, or car payment due—whatever you need . . ." Mr. Ross's voice trailed off as if he were sad to even mention such things, but Angela was beginning to feel that his words, his manner, and everything about him were well-rehearsed and finely honed.

"Again, thank you, Mr. Ross. I don't really need any financial help at this time."

"Well, I believe you have a fairly sizeable mortgage on this place—"

"Wait a minute, Mr. Ross. I don't want to be rude, but I'm not exactly sure what you're trying to do here this morning. I appreciate your condolences and your offering to help me financially, but I thought you came here to talk about my being a beneficiary of Kenny Chessin's insurance policy with your company."

"Did you know Kenny had a large life insurance policy?" Victor Ross asked.

"No, I didn't. He never told me, probably didn't want to worry me. Why do you ask?"

"I just wondered. Sometimes a young man will take out a large policy and tell his loved ones, and other young men won't tell anyone. Just curious . . . why would it have worried you if you had known Kenny had a large life insurance policy?"

"Mr. Ross, why don't you just tell me what is going on? Please respect me enough to be straightforward." Angela noticed a slight reddening of Mr. Ross's neck.

"Well, there is usually some delay in these kinds of accidental cases, some time for investigative work to occur, and while the beneficiaries are waiting for the case to settle, National Ways is more than willing to help cover expenses and bridge any financial gaps the beneficiaries might experience short-term."

"What is there to investigate?" Now Angela felt her own neck getting warmer.

"Lots of things, you know, the nature of the car crash, toxicology reports, the last date of a policy payment and things like that."

"Mr. Ross, I probably need to be getting ready for class. Any papers you want me to look over, you can just leave here on the counter. I'll call you if I have any questions," she said, conveying to the keenly perceptive Victor Ross her wariness.

"Well, that won't be necessary. If I could just get you to sign this one release form, I'm sure we can take care of everything," Victor said as if her signature were but a small, routine detail.

Angela began to read the form that was quite detailed and seemed anything but routine. She sat the form aside. "Mr. Ross, I must tell you that I won't sign this form or any other form from National Ways without legal counsel."

"But, Ms. Capelli—"

"That's it, Mr. Ross. I said I didn't want to be rude, but I take that back. I believe you have been polite on the surface but not so sensitive underneath. It looks to me like you've been trying to get me to sign some papers that I don't understand. You haven't really explained much to me, but I think you're trying to figure out a way for your company to save some money."

"But, Ms. Capelli, I can explain everything to you. I'm truly sorry. I know I've offended you when you're already upset."

"Thank you, Mr. Ross. I hope you are sincere in your apology. I'm young and inexperienced in matters like this, so I really do need to get some legal advice. I hope you understand. If you had a daughter my age, I'm sure you wouldn't want her to sign things unless she was comfortable."

"Well, thank you, Ms. Capelli. I truly am sincere in saying I'm sorry. Please call me after you've gotten whatever advice you need. I want you to be comfortable."

Mr. Ross left as unobtrusively as he had entered. Angela changed her mind and decided not to go to class. She stayed home and cried tears of sadness and tears she couldn't explain. She knew that she felt Kenny had really helped her grow up and learn how to take care of herself.

CHAPTER 78

"Angela, how are you, darling?" Red Conway's voice boomed over the phone like a voice from her past—the voice of a long-ago friend.

"I'm okay, Red. I'm doing okay."

"I'd love to take you to dinner any night you feel up to it." He didn't want to come on too strong, but he really missed Angela, and now that Kenny was gone, Red thought their relationship could be simple with fewer complications. He was thinking of inviting Angela to move in with him now that his wife was confined to a long-term care facility, with no prospects of ever coming home.

For a long time, Red had wanted his wife to be confined at home with around the clock nursing care, but it had become too depressing for him. He had reached a point where he dreaded coming home and seeing her lying there, helpless and deteriorating. This way, he could visit her regularly, which he knew he would do with dedication.

Red didn't want to rush things or scare Angela away.

"Red, I need to talk with you. I know you'd like to start up where we left off months ago, but I don't foresee that happening. It's not because you're not wonderful. You are. It's that we started our relationship in a way that wasn't really right. It wasn't right for either of us. You gave me money to spend time with you, which led to our ending up in bed together. And all the time, you were married. Two basically good people, but in order to be a couple, had to not think about obvious reasons why they shouldn't be together. Please just try to be my friend. I know you can be because you already have been. That's what I need—a friend who will give me some space to get over some of my past. Do you know what I'm saying?"

"Yes, I do, Angela. I really do," Red responded, unable to mask some of his disappointment in his voice. "Let me be a friend right now. Let me come and take you to lunch in a few minutes and listen. If you need a shoulder to cry on, I'm available."

"Good, that's very nice, Red. Pick me up whenever you're ready. I'll be waiting. And one thing I'll need is some advice."

"Advice about what?"

"Advice about how to find a good lawyer."

CHAPTER 79

Red was a perfect gentleman at lunch. They laughed occasionally, softly, and talked about everything from school to new cars. Red suggested the name of a lawyer, Leonard Harris, to help her deal with National Ways.

"It sounds to me like they're trying to manage down the claim," Red said.

"What does that mean?" Angela felt naïve.

"Kenny had a life insurance policy. National Ways sold him the policy and agreed to pay his beneficiaries in the event of his death, right?"

Angela nodded and listened closely.

"Well, if the policy was for a hundred dollars, let's say, and they can get by with paying you less money, say $75, they've managed the claim down by 25 % of its actual value."

"I see . . ."

"These insurance companies are all alike—they don't mind taking your money, but they really don't like to pay claims. People like Kenny buy a policy in good faith, and then when it's time to pay up, the insurance company tries to weasel out of it—low pay, slow pay, or no pay. That's their philosophy of managing claims. And this nerd Ross guy is really a deceitful little prick. He would love to get you to sign some papers releasing the company from paying 100 percent of what they owe you. Or he would like to drag the thing out for months, maybe even years, drawing interest on the money they should have paid you within forty-eight hours of Kenny's death."

"Damn, that's crazy. Another American institution undermined by corruption!" Angela was once again impressed by Red's street smarts and common sense. He spoke with authority.

"It's hard to say which came first, though, the insurance companies trying to take advantage of people or people trying to take advantage of insurance companies. But this guy Leonard Harris will set them straight. He's not a guy to fuck with, and I'm sure National Ways has heard of him. He's with a law firm in Downtown Columbus—Federer, Federer, Brush, and Felker. You ever hear of them?"

"No, not really," Angela admitted, feeling young and inexperienced in the ways of the world.

"They're a good firm, aggressive lawyers and well-connected. Allan Federer, their senior partner, did some work for me years ago, helped me set up dealerships in Florida. He's definitely a guy you don't want to get crosswise with. He's connected with the governor of Ohio and with the chairman of the Republican party in Washington. His father, Simon Federer, I knew personally years and years ago. Simon's still living at the ripe old age of eighty-eight but is no longer able to practice law. He's like an honorary partner. Most of my dealings in recent years have been with one of Federer's lieutenants, Bob Felker, who recommended Leonard Harris to handle your problem."

"Thanks, Red. You know I really appreciate this," the young woman said warmly.

"I know you do, Angela, and I'm thrilled to help you any way that I can. They'll just send the bill to me. Not to be nosey, but how much life insurance did Kenny have?"

"I have no idea, but I know I'm not the only beneficiary. I don't know if he has another living relative or not. He always told me he was an only child and that his dad had deserted him and his mom. He said he had lost touch with her and didn't know if she was alive. At the funeral, there were no relatives there—I didn't know who to contact."

"Well, I guess you'll find out how much insurance he had."

"Yeah, I will, Red. But regardless of how much, I want to pay for the lawyer. You've done too much for me from the beginning. I need to stand on my own two feet now."

CHAPTER 80

Leonard Harris was a very tall, slender man with a very receding hairline and thin hair on top. He combed all strands of his hair straight back, which fell in thick curls at the top of his starched collars. His bushy eyebrows partially hid behind horn-rimmed large glasses.

He was very intelligent, maybe brilliant, and extremely focused. He listened so intently to every word, every detail Angela provided that it made her somewhat nervous. She could understand that any opponent, be it another attorney or a claims adjuster, might be intimidated and feel as if they could neither keep up with nor outsmart Mr. Harris.

After their first meeting, Angela was mostly at ease and believed that Mr. Harris was probably the best attorney she could find. Her friend Red always seemed to come through.

Mr. Harris had already contacted National Ways and had the basic information that Mr. Ross had been so reluctant to share.

"Kenny took out a $1 million policy on his life and named you, your mom, and your sister as equal beneficiaries. He bought the policy seven months before his death, and the policy included a triple indemnity clause in the event of an accidental death. I think that is what the insurance company is balking about. They started trying to negotiate down the $3 million payment, saying that there was some indication that Kenny's death might have been intentional."

"You mean like a suicide?" Angela was trembling.

"Yes. Apparently, Kenny had some large gambling debts he was getting pressured to pay."

"I know that was true." Angela nodded.

"Well, I told Mr. Ross that his case was garbage and that National Ways had until the first of next month to pay us what they owed us or they would be facing a law suit for illegal business practices in the state of Ohio, plus a filing with the Department of Justice for unethical business conduct on a nationwide basis.

"Jesus, that must have scared little Mr. Ross." Angela still wanted to like Mr. Ross and believed he was just following orders from the company.

"I think so, but he didn't show it. He's been playing his role for so long that he can't break out of it. You know, the somewhat mousey, beat-around-the-bush, 'I'm sorry and just want to help' kind of role. He may even believe at this point that this is who he really is."

"I'm studying psychology, but I don't think they teach that kind of stuff in psych classes."

"Maybe not, but when you've been around people who are looking for money as long as I've been, nothing surprises you. People are capable of doing anything and then talking themselves into believing it was the right thing to do. At any rate, I will call you when I hear from National Ways, hopefully with good news—news that you can come back and pick up your check and that you, your mom, and your sister are all millionaires."

"Thanks, Mr. Harris. You're terrific. I'm sure glad you're on my side." Angela could only imagine if Mr. Harris worked for the insurance company, he would dig into Kenny's gambling, his debt to Mr. Werner and the Germans, and find out what she had done to pay off the debt.

Angela shook Mr. Harris's hand and left the law offices across the street from the State Capitol. She was extremely impressed with him and was looking forward to returning to his office.

On her next trip to see Mr. Harris, Angela would be even more impressed.

CHAPTER 81

Leonard Harris had called the receptionist at Federer, Federer, Brush, and Felker to let Angela know he was running late. Brenda, the plump middle-aged receptionist with slightly affected speech, greeted Angela with cool professionalism. Angela was accustomed to the majority of women being less than warm and friendly when they first met her. Kenny had said they were jealous of her beauty.

"Mr. Harris will be here within the hour, Ms. Capelli. He has been detained in court, waiting for a jury verdict.

Angela was sure Mr. Harris was not reluctant to perform in a courtroom; in fact, he probably relished it. He had said, though, that to take a large corporation to court was a last resort and that he would prefer to simply get the company to pay its debt, $3 million—not a small debt, but still a debt that National Ways owed to the Capelli women.

Angela's mom and sister in Southern Ohio had been visited by Victor Ross and had eagerly signed some papers, which Mr. Harris had retrieved to use as evidence of unethical business practices by National Ways.

The heavy double doors suddenly opened, and in walked two handsome men. Both were slender, physically fit, and clearly conveyed wealth and sophistication. The older man was probably in his early sixties and wore a perfect-fitting black suit with a subtle glen-plaid design and a crisp white shirt with elegant cufflinks. His vivid black-and-red striped tie coordinated with a black-and-red paisley pocket square.

The younger man also wore expensive clothes, though more casual ones. He wore beautifully tailored black slacks, a black-and-white small-checked sports coat, and a blue dress-shirt without a tie. His stylish black slip-ons gleamed.

"Hello, Donna—anyone looking for Mr. Morris or me?" the older man asked.

Angela sensed that the older gentleman was accustomed to having power and was probably in charge of some of the younger lawyers. Maybe this Mr. Morris was one of the lawyers, but no, he was probably a client. She didn't think the lawyers would come into the offices without a tie.

"Nothing for you, Mr. Morris—how *are* you?" Donna said, smiling a very friendly, welcoming smile to the younger gentleman. Almost before he responded with "I'm fine, Donna, and you?" she continued with "You have several messages, Mr. Federer, which Rose has put into your e-mail. And how was your lunch, sir?"

"Very good, too tempting, but we restrained ourselves—right, Austin?"

Both men laughed, looked to the side of the large reception area where Angela was sitting. Both smiled very cordially toward her and almost did a double take. Angela was accustomed to men staring at her and finding excuses to linger. "They're all thinking about what it would be like to have sex with you," Kenny used to say.

Mr. Federer, a man who had acquired some near-celebrity status in Angela's mind after lunching with Red, opened the door for Austin Morris and motioned for him to please enter first. Simultaneously, both men glanced back at Angela as if to make sure they had really seen what they thought they had seen.

But Angela was only interested in connecting with the younger man's glance. She could meet or look at Mr. Federer some other time. She was certain Mr. Harris could arrange an introduction. But this person named Austin Morris was the best-looking, seemingly good man she had ever seen. Kenny had frequently repeated Mae West's notorious line: "A good man is hard to find . . ."

When Angela's eyes met Austin's the second time he looked at her, both were pleased with what they saw. Austin saw an intelligent, incredibly lovely young lady, probably a law school student.

Angela saw a very handsome and refined man who was probably only a few years older than her. He seemed real smart, tuned in to the ways of the world. And she loved the way he looked at her. He conveyed kindness and seemed to be a supportive type of person. And she especially loved that his eyes did not convey that he was thinking about what it would be like to have sex with her.

CHAPTER 82

The next few weeks were a whirlwind. Leonard Harris had good news—National Ways produced three checks for $1 million each and a fourth check to cover his time and expenses.

"No need for you to have to pay out of your pocket just to get an insurance company to pay what it was obligated to pay all along," he told Angela as he gave her a perfunctory hug. *A fairly unemotional guy,* Angela thought. She had considered asking him if he knew a man named Austin Morris or if he would introduce her to Allan Federer. She had even come to the meeting thirty minutes early, hoping that she might see Austin Morris again.

But she did not.

"I would like to drive down to Gallipolis tomorrow to personally deliver the checks to your mom and sister. Would you like to go?" Mr. Harris asked. "Perhaps you could help them or advise them—most people don't get this much money all at once."

"Thank you, Mr. Harris. That would be very nice. I'll call them and tell them we're coming tomorrow. What time do you want me to come in tomorrow?"

"No, please. Let me pick you up. I've never driven by your condo (she knew he was referencing Victor Ross's comment), but I will find it. Is eight o'clock too early?"

"That's fine," Angela answered, mildly disappointed that she was not going to have another opportunity for a second chance meeting of Austin Morris. She would watch for him as she traveled around Columbus but was not confident that his travels took him to the places she went.

188

As she traveled out of Columbus, past Scioto Downs, through Circleville, and through Chillicothe, she became anxious. She felt hungry and nauseous at the same time. It couldn't be because of Mr. Harris—he was friendly, interesting, and a good listener. She liked that he was driving because his eyes couldn't bore in on her eyes and expressions as he listened.

"Are you too hot? Too cold?" He must have sensed her discomfort.

"No, I'm just not feeling good. Maybe I'm getting carsick."

"Do you want me to pull off so maybe you can get out and stretch, get some fresh air?"

"Oh god, no!" She saw an emotional reaction in Mr. Harris to her outburst.

"What's wrong, Angela? What's wrong?"

"Keep driving. Don't stop! I think this is probably the general area where Kenny crashed." She dropped her head into her hands, cried, and pulled tissues from her purse. Mr. Harris didn't know how to comfort her, so he kept driving.

Although suddenly very sad, Angela felt better.

It was good to see her mom and sister Katherine.

Just as they always were, they were elated to see her. Both of them admired Angela, and to their way of thinking, she had never made a mistake in her life. They wanted to believe she was perfect.

And now, as always, they were going to follow her advice. She was bringing them money that would change their lives and a big-time lawyer who was going to make sure their money grew and lasted forever. He had already made arrangements with one of the personal bankers at the Ohio Valley Bank to handle their accounts with his oversight.

Mrs. Capelli had had a few physical scares and was confronted by her doctor that she was killing herself. It was a struggle, but she was changing her lifestyle—she had totally stopped drinking, was attending AA ("I hate being around a bunch of drunks, but that's what I was," she would say), was exercising and trying to lose weight. She limited herself to five cigarettes a day but craved the twenty-five additional ones missing from her former pack-and-a-half-per-day habit.

This money would allow her to buy a new car, move to a new one-story home, and buy some exercise equipment. But the biggest thing the money would provide would be a sense of status. Having lived all these years in the undesirable area of Gallipolis, she was now going to move over to First Avenue, right on the river, where she could watch it panoramically every day.

Katherine was working at the Hair Apparent Beauty Salon in upper Gallipolis, on old Route 7 near the Silver Bridge. She had finally obtained her driver's license after three attempts and was hoping to obtain her beautician's license. Upcoming would be her second attempt. In the meantime, she was happy, washing hair, cleaning up the work areas, and helping out with some of the scheduling at the front desk. Katherine liked all her coworkers, and they liked her. Hair Apparent had a family atmosphere that customers enjoyed.

Katherine intended to buy a new car, lose some weight, and acquire a new wardrobe too. She knew she would have to restrain herself, to keep from buying new clothes before she lost the weight. Her mom had promised to help her.

The main thing Katherine wanted, which she had told Angela but not her mom, was breast augmentation. A "boob job," as she told Angela.

Angela didn't want to try to talk her out of it, but she suspected it would not change her sister as much as she hoped. She had never had any cosmetic surgery herself, but she suspected that the results did not always live up to people's expectations.

She knew in Katherine's case, she wanted to attract men, get married to one of them, and raise a family. Bigger boobs might not help, but Angela's focus was not on that. Instead, she simply tried to help Katherine break the news to their mom. They had agreed they would do it today together.

They would have to ask Mr. Harris to excuse himself for a few minutes.

CHAPTER 83

On the drive back to Columbus, Angela tilted her passenger's seat back and relaxed. She reflected on the successful day. Both her mom and Katherine had liked Mr. Harris, who had loosened his tie and rolled up his sleeves to be as down-to-earth as he could. He had sat at the kitchen table as if he had done so many times before. He helped them set up financial checks and balances to protect their long-term security and income and gave them all a gentle lecture about not spending money as if there were an endless supply.

"I've heard of people who get a big amount of money and waste it on friends, motorcycles, and all kinds of things. I can help you make wise decisions—tell your friends, who will come out of the woodwork, that before you can do anything, you need to talk to your attorney. That's what I'm here for."

Mr. Harris arranged for an investments person he had handpicked from the Ohio Valley Bank to work with Mrs. Capelli and Katherine on an ongoing basis.

And the talk about breasts was short and sweet. "I think you should get bigger boobs, honey," her mother had said. "I didn't know you wanted them, or maybe I would have figured out a way to give you part of mine."

CHAPTER 84

"Hello?" Angela answered the phone with an inexplicable touch of excitement.

"Is this Angela?" the mellow, reassuring voice asked.

"Yes, it is," she answered eagerly.

"My name is Austin. Austin Morris."

"Oh hello, Mr. Morris." *Oops,* she thought. She should have called him Austin.

"I don't know if you remember me—I saw you two weeks ago at the lawyer's office in Downtown Columbus. I was with Allan Federer. We walked in and talked for a moment to Brenda, the receptionist."

"Yes, I do remember you."

"I asked Allan to find out your number, which, being a stickler, he said he couldn't do. I later talked with Brenda, and she helped me out."

"That's fine, Austin. I'm impressed you were persistent. I remembered your name and thought about maybe trying to call you." *I might as well be honest,* she thought, although she didn't go on to tell him she had looked up his name and number on the Internet and had started to dial it a number of times.

"Well, I'm glad I beat you to the punch. I saw you and thought, 'Now there's someone I'd like to get to know,' and was wondering if you would like to go to dinner sometime?"

"I'm very flattered, Austin, and I really would like to do that . . ." Her voice trailed off.

"But? Are you dating someone?"

Angela liked the way he seemed to treat her with respect and not push her into something she might not want to do.

"I'm only hesitating because . . . because I might not be good company. I just lost my boyfriend."

"I'm sorry. I don't want to get in the way of a relationship like that," Austin offered sympathetically.

"No, it's not like that. It's not like he and I broke up and might get back together. He was killed in a car accident."

"Oh my. I'm so sorry. Maybe I should call you back in a few weeks and see how you're doing then," he volunteered.

"Don't wait that long, Austin. How about in a week?"

"I will definitely call you back in seven days from right now. Maybe I can help you. Maybe we can help each other."

"That sounds good . . . but I need to ask—have you recently lost someone too?"

"Yeah—a year ago next month. My wife passed away."

"I'm very sorry to hear that. How are you doing?"

"Pretty well, actually. Much better than I would have expected," Austin said clearly.

"That's good. Then there's hope. I'm sure I'll be much better a year from now and, hopefully, sooner."

"I hope so too, Angela. I will call you next week."

"That's good. That'll give me something to look forward to."

Both Austin and Angela knew that she really meant it.

Chapter 85

Austin and Angela were in love with each other.

From their first moment together, which they later debated—was it when they first saw each other at Allan Federer's law office, or was it when they first spoke on the phone, or was it on their first date?

Both of them felt very attracted to each other and wasted little time before freely exploring the relationship.

"I've only had two boyfriends, Austin. Kenny and an older gentleman, Red Conway. I'm not nervous about being here with you because I feel completely safe with you, not because I'm experienced or anything." It was their first date, and Angela had invited Austin into her condo and then into her bedroom.

"I feel safe with you too, Angela. I've dated quite a few girls—women—but I've never felt this way about anyone before."

After very satisfying though not elaborate or creative lovemaking, Angela returned to his comment. "What did you mean that you had never felt this way about anyone before? You must have felt that way about your wife, didn't you?"

"I loved my wife, whose name was Lorena, but we were close, more like good friends. I knew all about her first husband Len—how they met, how they lived their lives together, and everything. I knew her so well that we were intimate.

"With you," he continued while holding her, both propped up against her enormous pillows, "I feel as if we are intimate, as if maybe we lived our lives together in some other era."

"You mean like we were married or lived together in another lifetime and now we've been reincarnated?" Angela loved the way their minds seemed to imagine things along similar channels.

"Maybe, but not really. I just mean I don't know you as well as I knew Lorena, but I feel closer to you and more intimate with you."

"Perhaps it's because we're hoping to make love over and over." Angela lowered her head and began to kiss his nipples.

"I think you're right—I sure hope so," Austin responded with enthusiasm. He didn't want to tell her that he and Lorena had never made love, not even once. Nor did he mention or even want to think about the voracious sex he and Sasha had.

As the days and nights rushed by without seeming to end, the sheer beauty and exhilaration of their lovemaking seemed to trigger some guilt in him. He wondered why he had never made love to Lorena. He wondered if she had really wanted him to—no, he knew she had wanted him to. But then he wondered why she had never asked him to do so.

He became increasingly certain that he never wanted Angela to know that he had not made love with Lorena. This beautiful, breathtaking girl was very intuitive and quick to draw conclusions. He did not want her to conclude that he had married Lorena for her money—something that would not be uniquely her own conclusion.

There was some truth to that, but she wouldn't understand that it was really Lorena's idea, not his. But he could have said no or backed out. Maybe he had backed out emotionally and, therefore, had not addressed possible sexual needs in Lorena. For that, he felt some guilt as he thought back to his love and admiration for Lorena.

But when he thought about Angela, knowing this about him and Lorena or learning that he and Sasha had sex almost insatiably, he felt shame.

CHAPTER 86

Angela and Austin were inseparable. They went to Gallipolis and met Angela's mom and Katherine after a two-month intensive courtship. It didn't really feel like a courtship; rather, it felt more like a relationship they both had known existed and had finally found.

They talked; they communicated, sometimes with few words. A look, a touch many times spoke paragraphs.

"We're like a couple of old married folks," Angela said as their eyes met during a rare occasion of TV watching.

"Let's put an end to that kind of thinking," Austin said as he put his strong arm around her. "Let's start being a couple of young married folks."

"Are you sure?" Angela asked as her eyes welled up in joy. "I know you are sure, and so am I."

They began to plan their wedding, both of them knowing this was what they wanted since they had first seen each other.

Their parents met for the first time at the rehearsal dinner in Columbus. Austin had forewarned his parents and brother Nate that Angela's mother and sister were from humble roots and just recently had come into some money. That way, they were not surprised when they met the Capelli ladies but were secretly disappointed. They later talked with one another privately.

"Did you see how slovenly Angela's mom looked? How could someone as beautiful and pristine as Angela come from a mother like that?" Mr. Morris asked his wife.

"I don't really know, but let's try not to judge Angela based on her mother. She's delightful, extremely so, and I'm convinced she and Austin are going to have a beautiful life together," Mrs. Austin said while gently patting her husband and smiling reassuringly. She didn't want to get into the conversation she and her husband had had a few times about how Austin had never really had much of a marriage with Lorena. The age difference was too great, and the allotted time had been too short.

"You're right. You're right, honey," he agreed with his wife. "I'm glad Nate didn't follow up with Angela's sister after the wedding weekend was over. I know they were out all night together after the rehearsal dinner, and she couldn't keep her eyes off him at the wedding and the reception."

Neither knew that Nate and Katherine had actually spent the two nights together having sex, but they suspected. They knew that Nate was very experienced in bedding down women, and Katherine had seemed so attracted and so available to him.

Katherine had been feeling better about herself, having gained a great deal of money, and having lost a great deal of weight. But most importantly, she loved her new big breasts that jutted out and demanded attention.

Her sister's wedding was unforgettable, especially the night before when she had had her insatiable appetite for sex fully met. Nate was very experienced as she soon recognized. He was in total control of himself and of their melded bodies. He could hold off ejaculating almost indefinitely and did not stop after one time. She was a fast learner and did her best to keep up with him. She was well-prepared for the second night and more than satisfied Nate.

"Are you disappointed Nate hasn't called or e-mailed you since Angela's wedding?" her mother asked Katherine sensitively two months later.

"Sort of . . . but I think he will. I don't think he'll ever find someone who'll be as good for him as I could be."

"That's good, honey. I'm so glad you're not hurt . . . not hurt and rejected," Katherine's mother responded. "You can always change your mind and try to call him . . ." She looked at her nearly-beautiful daughter. Katherine would never come close to Angela looks-wise, but she certainly had grown in confidence and seemed to feel pretty good about herself. Ever since the plastic surgery, Katherine had a new outlook on life and was constantly being asked out by boys from Gallipolis and Point Pleasant.

"I don't think I'm gonna call him, Mom. I really don't. But you know what?"

"What, honey?"

"If Nate never realizes what he missed out on, that's okay. But someday if he does and he comes to find me, maybe I'll be married, and it'll be tough shit for him!"

Katherine arched her back and looked at herself from top to bottom in the full-length mirror of their new home on the Ohio River. "That'll be just fine because my husband will discover what Nate missed."

PART VI

Chapter 87

Austin wondered why he had agreed to meet this woman, Janie Rosen, from Boca Raton as he drove to his office in Pelican Marsh. He had a lot on his mind as usual as he made the left hand turn off Immokalee and headed south on Tamiami Trail.

The trail from Tampa to Miami, he thought. *Probably no one ever drove from Tampa all the way to Miami on this road, Route 41, anymore.*

It was a few minutes before eight, and he had plenty of time to get organized before the Rosen woman came to see him at ten. He could get caught up with Christina, his executive assistant, have her respond to his e-mails and texts and make some calls on his behalf.

"Good morning, Austin!" Christina always greeted him with the same positive mood and had never gone through an awkward phase in which she forced herself to call him Austin instead of Mr. Morris. Austin appreciated her upbeat attitude, her wit, and her uncomplicated ways of dealing with him. Many people seemed to be a bit stilted in relating to him, almost as if they were afraid of him or of his wealth and power.

"Hi, Christina—and how are you?"

"Just fine, Austin. I have your bagel and coffee waiting for you."

"Oh thanks, Christina. Anything urgent going on?"

"Only if you and Mr. Federer have some urgent topic to discuss. He called at seven thirty, didn't want to distract you on your cell phone, and asked that you call him when you arrive and get settled."

"Good. I'll call him in a few minutes."

Christina was an exceptional assistant, in part because she was very smart and could read people extremely well. She could sense by their inflections on the phone and their body language in person what their character and intentions were.

And she could read Austin very well. He tried to mask strong emotions, particularly negative emotions—she knew that. She thought he seemed to want to be above all that—the pain and suffering of the middle class.

She recognized some negative reactions in him today as soon as she mentioned Allan Federer's call about wanting to speak to him this morning. She knew Mr. Federer wanted to talk with Austin well in advance of the appointment at ten o'clock with Ms. Rosen, the mysterious Janie Rosen. Christina hadn't figured out who she was or what her connection was with Austin. Maybe she knew some dirt about the squeaky-clean Austin Morris and was going to blackmail him. Christina hoped not; Austin was an exceptionally good boss and a very generous one too. Sometimes, though, she found it a little hard to believe or accept that he was as pure or righteous or even perfect as he came across as being.

Apparently, Austin himself was unclear about what Ms. Rosen wanted, but apparently, Mr. Federer, always the shrewd Jewish lawyer, had advised Austin to meet with her. He probably knew at least part of what she wanted.

Christina read Austin's facial squint, along with a slight uplifting of his eyebrows to convey that he had some anxiety about the ten o'clock meeting, not exactly dread but anxiety, anxiety perhaps about what this woman would want from him or about what he might find out from her.

Chapter 88

"Good morning, Allan. How's everything?"

"Fine, Austin. Thanks for calling me back. How are Angela and the baby?"

"Oh, they're fine, really great. Samantha's just starting to crawl, and Angela's busy being a philanthropist, social chairperson, and hotshot golfer."

"That's good. Give her my best. How's your golf game?"

"Not too bad. I keep flirting with a single-digit handicap, but I can't seem to reach it."

"You need to play some easier courses. Tiburon and Naples National don't help."

"I know, I know . . ." Austin's voice trailed off as he anticipated Allan was ready to get to the purpose of his call.

"Austin, I want to talk to you about Janie Rosen, who I understand is going to be seeing you a little later this morning."

"Okay. Yes, I'm scheduled to see her at ten."

"I thought about flying down last night so that I could give you some of this news in person, but given our relationship, I thought we could make a telephone call work for us."

"Oh, sure, Allan. And you know I trust your judgment . . . but I'm getting worried because your voice sounds so ominous."

"Well, sit down, take a deep breath, and then exhale."

Austin didn't say that he was already sitting and he endured the pause.

Allan Federer continued, "This Janie Rosen is related to your first wife, Lorena."

"How? How so?" Austin was puzzled why this apparently was a bad thing. Maybe the Rosen woman wanted money or had some claim to part of Lorena's estate.

"Well, actually. . ." Allan paused again, which previewed the rest of what he had to say. "Janie is Lorena's daughter."

"What? How could that be?" Clearly, Austin was shocked.

"I know it's upsetting, but let me explain. I know it's hard for you, Austin, but Lorena was a beautiful young Jewish girl in Cleveland years ago and was seen by many as 'the prettiest girl in Shaker' during that time. Exactly what happened or how it happened is uncertain, but Lorena became pregnant. Given the strictness of her parents who were nearly orthodox Jews, she had but one choice—have the baby and give it up for adoption." Allan let out a breathy sigh, glad to have unburdened himself by sharing this information.

"I don't know what to say, Allan. It's crazy. I guess anything is possible . . ." Austin's mind was racing forward. How could his beloved Lorena, the woman who had taught him so much and given him an unbelievable start in life, keep a secret like this from him?

He immediately thought of those conversations they had had about openness and knowing each other. He remembered how she had insisted that no one really knows another person in this life, only oneself. He had disagreed with her and had even pointed to their own relationship as a case in point as clearly refuting her claim.

Now, years later, now that she was gone, her belief was crazily verified. If she were alive now, she would say, "See, I told you, darling. You only *think* you know someone. In fact, they only let you know what they want you to know."

But if she were alive, she would never say essentially, "I told you so." Instead, she would say that she regretted he had found out, particularly in this way. Then she would probably ask how this really had any bearing on who they were today or how they felt about each other.

"I wonder if Len knew," Austin muttered aloud, actually to himself.

"I don't know," Allan responded, still listening on the other end of the phone. "I doubt that he did."

Austin wondered why Allan took that position, although it probably wasn't important. If anything, Allan probably wanted Austin to get through this difficult news and not get hung up about why Lorena hadn't told him of her past and what it might mean if she had told her first husband but not her second.

Austin knew that Allan wanted him to move through this quickly, even pragmatically, so if nothing else, he would be in good mental shape to meet with this woman who in some sort of strange way could actually be his stepdaughter. A stepdaughter he never knew and, until seconds ago, never knew existed. A stepdaughter who was older than him. The whole thing felt strange and not in a fascinating way. Austin knew he needed to guard against getting upset when he hastily said he would call Allan later, and now it was apparent why.

"I sure as hell don't want to get pissed off," he said aloud, and this time, Allan was no longer on the phone. Austin went into his private bathroom and felt as if he were going to throw up and have diarrhea at the same time. Neither occurred.

CHAPTER 89

At five minutes after ten, there was an entrance made to his outer office. He heard Christina greet the guest and then walk toward his office door. He met her as she approached the door and heard her say, "Ms. Rosen is here to see you." With that, she rolled her eyes and smiled to convey that this Ms. Rosen was an attractive female.

Austin looked beyond Christina to get his first look at the visitor and extended his hand to shake hers. He was immediately struck by her good looks and by the way she carried herself. Janie Rosen was reasonably tall, somewhat slender, and a woman who stood with erectness. She was ill at ease, he could tell. She was confident in her abilities, in what she wanted to do but, beneath the surface, seemed very self-conscious.

"Good morning, Mr. Morris. I'm Janie Rosen."

Austin had thought about "playing dumb" as if he didn't know what Allan Federer had told him. As if he didn't know that Janie was claiming to be Lorena's daughter. But when he saw her, he instantly decided to be open and straightforward. Maybe it wasn't even a decision; it just seemed like the only way to be.

With such a lovely, beautiful woman like this who instantly reminded him of Lorena, to play games seemed like a deeply dishonest thing to do.

"Janie, call me Austin. I've been looking forward to meeting you." Just after deciding to be honest, he felt himself not telling the truth. In fact, he had been dreading the thought of meeting her.

"You have?" Janie responded with dark eyes flashing. Dark eyes that seemed to see deeply into him. Dark eyes capable of ice and of heat that had experienced both pain and joy. Dark eyes that did not accept any wool being pulled over them.

"Well, actually, looking forward to it but with some anxiety," Austin corrected himself.

"I know what you mean," she reacted with an alluring kind of nervousness.

Janie Rosen seemed very vulnerable, even needy, Austin thought. She may look a lot like her mother but without the quiet confidence and poise. Lorena had always seemed so strong, so self-assured, even as she faced the certainty of imminent death.

"How can you know what I mean? Are you a mind reader?" Austin felt himself trying to lighten the mood and knew that he was experiencing an agitating combination of feelings—he felt both sorry for her and attracted to her. Even when he had known Lorena was dying, he hadn't quite felt sorry for her.

In hindsight, though, he had had twinges of sorrow, guilt, or pity as he reminisced about his brief marriage. These feelings all seemed to revolve around his not having made love to her, especially after he eventually concluded she probably wanted him to.

"No, but I read people pretty well. I'm trained as a social worker. To help people, I need to be able to understand them." Janie's dark eyes seemed to light up in response to Austin's attempt to change the mood. Or was it that she was in some way trying to flirt with him? Austin wondered but then began to think about Angela.

How could he be feeling so attracted to another woman just on the heels of having made love that morning to his adorable, adoring wife? Angela was probably the nicest, most selfless, and caring person he had ever known. The way she demonstrated unconditional love and patient love for Samantha was so reassuring to him. Reassuring that he had made a very solid although fairly quick decision in his second trip to the altar.

There were some things about Angela's past that were murky or unclear, but until recently, such things had not been of concern to Austin. He knew that he loved her and that Angela was a very good, very wholesome person who would do anything for him and for Samantha.

Exactly what her past life had been seemed fairly straightforward. Like everyone, she had probably done some things she was embarrassed about or ashamed of, but who hadn't? The boyfriend Kenny sounded like a guy with a lot of issues, and he must have been some kind of control-freak, apparently a very fast driver too.

Her mother and sister seemed like okay people—not very sophisticated, but basically salt-of-the-earth people. He suspected their having been big benefactors of Kenny's insurance policy had not changed them much. They both looked up to Angela and thought she could do no wrong. And they had been very accepting and welcoming to him.

But this business the other night with Fredrik Werner had been more than unsettling. It had been very bothersome and worrisome to Austin. He was certain that Angela and Fredrik recognized each other and that whatever had happened between them was something Angela did not want to discuss.

The fact that Werner had called her by her middle name, Marie, was extremely unnerving to Austin. Had she lived some type of double life before he knew her? The odds of someone calling a beautiful woman by her middle name and never having actually interacted with her seemed infinitesimally low.

No, he was sure that Angela and Fredrik had had some sort of encounter in the past. It had bothered him, and he had thought about engaging a private investigator to find out what had happened, but he had decided to wait.

He had decided to wait because he had wanted to take on the more pressing concern—who was this Janie Rosen, and what did she want? Today he was finding out unbelievable information very, very rapidly. Now that she was here face-to-face and seeming almost mysterious, he found himself rapidly losing interest for the moment in trying to find out the details, possibly sordid ones, of Angela's past.

He loved Angela, he loved Samantha, and he loved the life they had together as a little family. He didn't want anything to spoil it.

But he knew, as he stared into the emotional, almost smoldering eyes of Lorena's daughter, that this was a woman who could spoil things for him.

CHAPTER 90

The morning went by fast, and Austin learned quite a bit about Janie. She had been raised by Harry and Elinor Rosen in Shaker Heights. Her father was deceased, and her mother Elinor suffered from Alzheimer's and received round-the-clock care over in Boca.

Janie had learned the truth about her birth mother, Lorena, from Allan Federer. Sometime earlier, Elinor had written a letter to Janie, telling her that she was, in fact, adopted. Allan's father, Simon Federer, had arranged the private adoption.

After Janie contacted Allan Federer, he apparently had extracted the information about her birth from his father Simon. All records had been destroyed, but Simon Federer had remembered the details with uncanny clarity. The only detail he did not know or could not recall was who the baby's biological father was. Perhaps he had never been identified.

"Do you have time for lunch?" Austin suddenly asked at eleven forty-five. Surprising himself, he felt almost desperate inside. He didn't want this lovely lady, so much like her mother but so different, to leave.

He wanted to be with her, to have lunch with her, and maybe to spend the afternoon with her. He could easily get a motel room at the Registry, the Ritz-Carlton, or even use one of the guest rooms included in his membership fee at Naples National. He was very aroused and felt that he wanted to make love to Janie—but knew that he shouldn't.

Exactly why he was so drawn to her wasn't clear. The feeling was shocking to him as he had not felt this kind of desire, especially so immediately, since he had first seen Angela. Could the love at first sight phenomenon apply to more than one person?

Was he really in love with Angela? Or was he attracted to Janie because she might be a thrilling release and a way of paying back Angela for keeping secrets from him?

Yet Lorena had kept an even bigger secret from him. She had had a baby as a youngster and had given her up for adoption. What kind of person could actually do that? He thought of Samantha and the depth of love and commitment he and Angela had for her. How could anyone walk away from that?

And Lorena had seemed so calm, so certain of herself, and so without guilt. Had time healed all her misgivings and doubts? Why had she and Len not had any children? How could Lorena, knowing she would die and leave behind an incredible fortune, not bother to try to find out what had become of her baby girl—her only child—and leave something to her?

"I can have lunch, but I will need to head back to Boca right afterward," Janie responded with eyes sparkling. It was as if she knew what Austin was fantasizing about and just might be willing to consider an afternoon together in a hotel, but not today.

"I'll have Christina make us a reservation at the Registry. There's a special table there where we can look out onto the gulf and forget where we are."

"Well, just as long as we don't forget who we are," Janie said with a degree of seriousness that seemed to be a warning to both of them.

Christina responded instantly when Austin buzzed her to come in and make a luncheon reservation for them. Surely, she hadn't been hovering close to his closed office door, trying to eavesdrop. He needed to check out just how soundproof his office was, Austin thought to himself.

"Of course, Austin. At the Registry, I presume?" Christina asked in a way that suggested she too had been his luncheon companion at the special table.

"Sure, Christina," Austin answered.

Christina gave the slightest squint of her eyes as she looked first at Janie and then at Austin. Austin was confident that he read her unspoken message correctly: "Be careful."

"She is protective of you, isn't she?" Janie asked as Christina closed the door.

"Yes, I think so," Austin answered.

"She seems like a very good person," Janie continued. "Is she from here?"

"Actually, she's from Miami. Her parents were from Puerto Rico, and she lived in Miami before coming over here. I think she has a large family, lots of brothers and sisters, and wanted to get a little space or distance away from them."

Austin liked the way he could communicate with Janie, especially in the areas of people and human feelings. It was evident that she knew a lot about these subjects, and he liked the way she made him feel as if he were astute himself in these matters.

They had wasted little time in getting to the subject of Janie being Lorena's daughter. After brief initial awkwardness, Austin had blurted out, "I'm sorry you never knew Lorena, your mother."

"I am too, I guess. I've read about and even been exposed to people who were adopted and who spent a big part of their lives searching for their biological mother or father. I guess I'm different in that during my whole life, I never knew I was adopted. This mission to find my biological mother is only a few days old, and I somehow felt at the outset I would not find her alive."

"How can I help you, Janie? What can I do?" Austin didn't know if he was cringing on the inside because he was feeling that she might be grasping for a big chunk of money or, on the other hand, that he might want to be generous and give her a modest chunk of money.

"I guess, without being snoopy, I'd like to know what kind of person she was. Was she good? Was she not so good? Did she have quirky little habits or idiosyncrasies? I really don't want to pry into your relationship with her. I just really want to know who my biological mother really was. I guess it's like discovering that there was someone on this earth who may have stepped on the same sidewalks in Shaker Heights that I did years later who was my flesh and blood mother. I just want to learn as much as I need to learn about her."

With that said, Janie began to cry without shedding tears. Austin knew her hurt was deep.

"You said you want to learn as much as you need to learn about her. Maybe you want to learn as much as you possibly can about her. Then you can try to forget those things that you don't want to remember." Austin wanted to be supportive and to reassure Janie that she was on a mission that would be helpful. He embraced her as they stood to leave his office and go to lunch.

He felt unnerved by her reaction—she hugged him as if she loved him. She squeezed him tightly, and her soft but firm body seemed to meld into his. For a few seconds he felt as if they were one.

Austin felt as though Janie was drawing strength from his body. He felt as if he were genuinely helping her in a way that he couldn't define. By helping her, even though he felt strength draining from his body, he seemed to be helping himself.

Janie reminded him of Lorena when he closed his eyes.

CHAPTER 91

Lunch at the Registry lasted for two hours. The panoramic view took them far away.

Without exaggerating, Austin described Lorena as one of the most wonderful women he had ever known.

"She was deeply caring, very sensitive, and capable of intense companionship. I think she and her first husband Len had one of the greatest love affairs of all times—one that never became stale. Their marriage was an adventure together—the two of them traveled, worked, and tried new things. They did everything, I mean everything, together.

"Do you think she adapted to Len, or did he adapt to her?" Janie asked, in some ways thinking about her own failed relationships.

"I think the answer is no and no," Austin responded. "I think they became a couple, a unit, without either of them sacrificing or adapting. It probably sounds strange or cliché, but I believe each of them benefited from the other. Each of them expanded without having to give up anything, any aspect of themselves."

"I spend a great deal of time with couples, providing counseling aimed at helping them learn how to get along—how to communicate, how to solve problems together, and how to enjoy each other," Janie said.

"I guess my biological mother and her husband would never have needed that kind of help," she concluded.

"No, not really," Austin agreed. "They could have written the book on marriage."

"When people say, including counselors like me, that to have a good marriage, two people really have to work at it—that must not always be the case," Janie reflected rhetorically.

"It's probably true for the vast majority of us humans, but Len and Lorena operated at a whole other level," said Austin. "I must admit that I learned an unbelievable amount of life's information from Lorena. I grew, but I don't think I ever achieved the same level of wisdom as Lorena."

"That's because you're considerably younger, with far fewer life experiences than she. You are an outstanding person for your age—excuse me—" Janie suddenly stood up and almost threw her napkin onto the special table.

Austin was stunned and felt upset because she was upset. "Did I say something wrong? I'm sorry. I know this is probably very difficult, very upsetting . . ."

"No, I just don't want to delve into your relationship with her. I don't want to know what you two did together. It's none of my business, and I have no right to judge you. Besides, I need to find the ladies room."

Before Austin could point toward the restrooms, she was gone and headed in the right direction. He decided to go to the men's room himself.

He discovered that he was partially aroused as he stood at the urinal. His urine was slow in coming. What was it about this woman that triggered his desire? Was it just lust, which was a huge component in his relationship with Sasha? Was it that Janie was a seductive, younger version of Lorena?

He even wondered if his sexual reactions to Janie were really reactions to Lorena and had something to do with his beliefs that he really should have made love to Lorena, especially while she had been well enough to enjoy it maybe even back before they got married.

As Austin left the men's room, he was struck by how dark the alcove for both restrooms was. Two large traditional oil paintings hung over top of each other, bordered by flickering lighted sconces. He leaned forward and tried to make out the figures in the paintings. Two scenes of a fox hunt, dotted with red jackets of the equestrians, and more difficult to distinguish brown and white hounds.

Austin knew he was lingering in the alcove, hoping that Janie would soon appear. He felt the same sudden need for sex that he had felt when Sasha first interviewed for the job at VC. He had tried to forget about Sasha, but sometimes her smell, her body, and her unrelenting quest for passion reappeared in his fantasies.

Janie reappeared. She came from the ladies' room, seemingly in a rush, hopefully to get back to see him, he thought. He noticed that she had used her fingers or a pick to tousle her riveting black curly hair. Her heated aroma instantly conveyed that she had applied some fresh perfume. *Wonderful,* he thought.

They collided like soft magnets, passionately kissing and locking themselves together. Neither was even aware of a possibility that others might see them. They were alone, just the two of them, on an island where no one else mattered.

CHAPTER 92

"We had better stop," Janie said in a husky voice untinged by guilt. "Even though it's you, they might think we disappeared without paying for lunch."

"Let's hope not," Austin said, wondering whether they had clung to each other for one minute or five minutes.

"Aha, our special table is still here," Janie remarked, smiling as Austin helped her get reseated. She unfolded and put back the fresh replacement napkin the server had provided during their absence on her lap.

"I'm glad you liked the table," Austin offered.

"I loved the table, I loved our conversation, and I loved our time together. But I really should go."

"You can't go yet—we're not finished," Austin seemed to be pleading.

"We may never be finished, Austin. But we have done a lot, a lot more than I ever thought about. I really appreciate your telling me so much about my biological mother. I'm sorry I never knew her when she was alive. I know that as I think about her and analyze the information you've given me as I will, it will be very helpful, very calming to me."

"But you've never answered my important question," Austin said.

"You mean the one about what can you do to help me?" Janie looked him squarely in the eyes and seemed to know him better than he really wanted to be known.

"Yes, exactly," he answered.

"I really can't think of anything—I think you've already helped me by telling me what a good and decent person my biological mother was and even validating it by demonstrating what a good and decent person you, her second husband, are."

"But, but . . ." Austin started to question his own decency and refer to the passionate exchange in the alcove.

"No buts, no regrets. We did what we wanted to do and, probably, what we needed to do. We stopped before we went further than one of us might have wanted to go. We learned some things, but it may take us a while to figure out just what they are," she said as she stood, waiting for him to walk with her to the valet stand.

Austin felt okay. He made small talk as they drove back to the office.

"I will just get in my car here," Janie said as they pulled into the parking lot.

"Don't you want to come back upstairs?" Austin asked, sounding to himself as though he asked it feebly.

"Yes, but I won't. I really need to get home and see my real mother, the only one I will ever know. And I think Christina will be happier if you come back alone. She really does want to protect you, you know."

"Yeah, yeah. But when can I see you again?"

"Whenever you want, but wait a little while."

"Why? How long?" Austin's voice reflected worry—worry that he might not get to see her again.

"Long enough for both of us to think about what we're doing." Janie suddenly seemed very calm and in complete control of her feelings.

"All right. That's good. I understand," Austin replied, wanting to kiss her perfect, somewhat pouty lips again.

But he sensed she didn't want that, so he settled for her kissing his forehead. "You're special, Austin," Janie Rosen whispered as she gave him one more glimpse of her passionate, ice-hot eyes.

Chapter 93

Soon after the Naples Charity Ball, Angela Morris called Fredrik Werner. She felt silly, calling from a pay phone. Somehow, she imagined that Austin might check up on her and look at her cell phone records.

She had never cheated on Austin and knew that she never would. She would never engage in some type of affair or secret sexual encounter. That had all ended when Kenny was killed.

Her behavior changed drastically when he died, along with some of her thinking. The whole business about sex being one thing and making love being something else all seemed like some kind of mind game Kenny was playing. "He really was like some kind of pimp," Angela concluded. He wanted her to love only him, be loyal to him, and do whatever he told her to do.

He farmed her out like a high-class prostitute, not only to make money but also to feed his ego. He could convince himself that this woman loved him so much that she would allow herself to be subservient to him. She would escort other men, fuck them if they wanted, but then save her "true love" feelings only for Kenny.

"I must have been young and stupid," she told herself. "Definitely naïve."

Kenny had not been so brilliant either, she thought. She grimaced as she recalled their past. She probably had loved him at one time as much as she as a teenager was capable of loving, but that love had eroded as her respect for him had declined.

In their latter months together, she believed she had mostly felt sorry for him.

But leaving the money to her, her mother, and her sister had mostly redeemed Kenny in Angela's eyes.

"This is Fredrik Werner." The voice from her past, a few years ago during the long night at the University Inn, had not changed. She vividly remembered that night and the morning after as well as the recent evening at the fund-raiser with embarrassing shame.

"Fredrik, this is Angela. You knew me as Marie."

"Oh my god! How are you? Thank you for calling."

"You're welcome, Fredrik. I wanted you to know that I'm sorry I acted as if I didn't remember you the other night. I hope you understand—I'm married now, have a young daughter, and I don't want secrets from my past to upset my perfect little life."

"Oh yes, yes, yes. I am sorry too. I was just so surprised and happy to see you and to see how beautiful you still are."

"Thank you, Fredrik. You look well too. You look happy, and I know you have a fantastic wife in Joan."

"You're right. Joan is fabulous. I am a lucky man. I never thought I deserved someone as pretty, as smart, and as refined as Joan. I think you really helped me back at Ohio U. You were the first really decent girl I ever went out with."

"That's nice of you to say, Fredrik. Thanks. But let me ask you something—are you okay if we never tell our spouses about our time together back in college?"

"Oh yes, absolutely! I know it would not help either of us. And it would not help your husband or Joan."

"Good. Then let's just put that night in Athens behind us and strike it from our memories."

"I don't know if I can agree to strike it from my memory, but I give you my word—I will never tell Joan or anyone about our unbelievable night together back then."

"That's fine. That's all I need. I do appreciate it, Fredrik, and I know you're a man of your word," Angela responded very positively. She wanted to believe Fredrik was totally honorable, but she didn't really know for sure.

"Most definitely, Angela. I just can't promise that I won't remember our night together because I know I will. Sometimes even when I'm umm . . . very involved with Joan, I'm thinking about you."

"Please don't tell me that, Fredrik. I'm going to try to forget you said that. I'm going to try real hard. Joan is a wonderful person, and she deserves all your love and focus."

"You're right. I agree. I promise to never say anything. I just want you to know that my night with you was the most beautiful night of my life. You were the first woman I ever loved, and Joan was the second."

After their goodbyes, Angela hung up the phone and felt partially reassured. She believed Fredrik and believed that he would never with forethought reveal their secret. But what if he and Joan had a fight or even split up? Might he tell her on the spur of the moment to hurt her and as a way of destroying the friendship Joan and Angela might have?

Probably best to keep the relationship with the Werners more one of acquaintances than one of bosom buddies. That wouldn't be hard to do because she was sure that Fredrik was not Austin's type. About all they had in common, really, was lots of money. But then too, both of them had been in bed with her. That seemed weird. *What a small world,* she thought.

As she thought further about Joan Werner, she decided that breaking up with Fredrik would probably be one of the last things Joan would ever want to do. The lifestyle and sheer wealth would be hard to walk away from. Plus, Angela was convinced that Joan really loved Fredrik. And he loved her.

Maybe someday, Angela thought, *I would tell Austin a little bit more about my past.* But she didn't think she could ever tell him everything. What good would that do? What purpose would that serve?

She had already told him that she had traveled with and had been somewhat involved with Red Conway. She hadn't gone into detail about all the money Red had spent on her and the strong sexual relationship the two of them had enjoyed. Austin, like most people in the Columbus area, knew who Red Conway was. He had seen the tanned, white-haired, silver-tongued car dealer pitching his products on Columbus television stations. And then, as if that weren't enough, Austin saw him frequently on Fort Myers television stations, inviting people to come into his "stores" in South Florida.

Angela concluded that Austin had sort of written Red Conway off as an old man, a "sugar daddy" with whom Angela spent time because Kenny and Red were friends. He seemed to assume that Red probably had just wanted cute young girls to hang around with him, consistent with the image of a powerful, aging playboy. It didn't seem to occur to Austin that Red Conway was amazingly virile, like a man half his age.

That was fine, but little did he know . . . Angela was confident she would never be quizzed about whether or not she and Red had enjoyed sex together—Austin apparently believed, or wanted to believe, that they hadn't. And Angela totally trusted Red. After all he had done for her, including the way he had been there when she really needed him, she knew her past was safe with Red.

Two months earlier, Red had called Angela to see if they could get together some afternoon in Naples. He was still traveling back and forth frequently and now owned a Gulfstream himself. His wife had passed away, and he wanted to see her.

Just as she had now explained to Fredrik, she had told Red that she did not want to return to the past and thought they both should put their old relationship behind them.

Red had said he understood perfectly and had in no way made her feel uneasy as Fredrik had. "You will always know how to find me," Red had concluded their conversation.

In spite of Red's philandering way of life, Angela trusted him. Intuitively, he seemed honorable, even though his behavior was somewhat at odds with what Angela felt in her heart. Maybe he was the father figure that had been snatched away from her so early in her life. It probably helped that she had never met his wife, and therefore, the "victim" had no real identity or seemed not to have ever existed.

Angela just knew that she trusted Red more than she trusted Fredrik to keep the past hidden.

She knew that Austin had been bothered by the fact that Fredrik recognized her at the social event. Even though the interaction seemed to pass right by Joan, Angela knew that Austin perceived that Fredrik's response was valid. Austin probably was very curious about why Fredrik had called her Marie.

"If he asks me, I'll tell him, 'I met Fredrik at a fraternity party at Ohio University. There was a lot of drinking. My girlfriend and I had planned to go, and then she backed out at the last minute. I used the name Marie because I didn't want someone to know my real name, as I was living with Kenny. Yes, I sort of cheated on Kenny, and it was wrong. I had been thinking about breaking up with him, but I didn't really have the guts to tell him yet. Then he had the fatal car crash. I'm sorry. It was terrible, but please don't judge me today based on my past. I guess we all have some skeletons in our closets. I'm just sorry you learned about mine in this way. And above all else, please don't see this as having anything to do with us. I love you like I've never loved anyone before. The only person I sort of felt love for in the past was Kenny, but it was not a healthy love like you and I have. I will never do anything dishonest in our relationship, Austin . . . please believe me."

She had rehearsed her answer to Austin's questioning in her mind. She was satisfied with her answer but hoped to God he never asked.

CHAPTER 94

"How did you make out with the Rosen woman?" Allan Federer asked Austin.

Interesting choice of words, Austin thought as he answered, "Just fine. She's really a nice, sincere person. Tell me again how she found out she was adopted and how she found out Lorena was her real mother."

"Her mother, the one who raised her, has Alzheimer's and, a couple of years ago, left a letter to be opened if she ever became mentally incapacitated. Eventually, her mother got worse and worse, and a couple of weeks ago, Janie Rosen opened the letter. In it, her mother, Elinor Rosen, told her she was adopted and later told her that the birth mother was a young unmarried girl named Lorena Wasserman. The private adoption was arranged through my father Simon. Janie Rosen contacted me, looking for my father. I told her that Dad was retired but that I would find out all that I could."

"You checked it out with your dad?" Austin queried.

"I did, and even though he's not as sharp as he used to be, he remembered the situation well. He arranged for the Wasserman family to give up their baby girl, Janie, and he placed her with the Rosen family. The Wassermans were satisfied, the Rosens were thrilled, and supposedly everyone lived happily ever after."

"You mean they were living happily ever after until Janie opened up her mom's letter," Austin remarked.

"Exactly. The Wassermans and Rosens never knew each other, and apparently, the Wassermans were able to hide the fact that their daughter had a baby. No offense, Austin, but I'm surprised Lorena didn't come forward and maybe try to find her daughter."

"You can imagine how shocking that is to me. To be blunt, I inherited a fortune from Lorena, and I'm amazed that after she knew she was dying, she wouldn't have tried to locate and leave something to her long-lost daughter, especially since I always thought that Lorena was such a wonderful, caring, and generous person. Maybe she had a side to her that I never saw."

"I'm no shrink," Allan continued, "but I think different people handle problems differently. Some cover up problems by lying and denying. Some just shut them off. It's like Lorena as a young girl had a terrible chapter in her life story, but once she got through it, she closed it and never went back to read it again."

"How could anybody—least of all Lorena—do something like that?" Austin asked plaintively.

"Lord, I don't know. I guess she thought it best to put that chapter, that trauma behind her and never to tell anyone."

"She must have told Len, don't you think?" Austin wondered why he was so interested in the answer to the question.

"No, I'm sure not. Len and I were very close, and I'm sure he would have brought it up with me."

"You can never be sure," Austin countered. "Lorena and I were extremely close for years, and she never brought it up with me. Maybe Len knew but didn't want to ask you about it."

"I don't believe that. Len was absolutely one of the shrewdest businessmen I've ever known and totally committed to accumulating wealth and preserving it. If he had had any hint that Lorena might have an heir out there somewhere, he would have been all over it. He would have had me doing investigative research, finding the person, and figuring out how we could protect the estate against any claims she might have on it." Allan's voice of certainty was convincing.

"That's very interesting. I guess I should be thinking about what if Janie makes a claim against the estate now that it's mine. I don't know if she needs money, but most people wouldn't mind having more money than they already have," Austin said.

"I think Lorena crossed that bridge in her mind. If she had just left the estate to you as a close friend, someone like Janie could come out of the woodwork and lay claim against the estate. But the fact that you and she were married and consummated the relationship makes it next to impossible for someone, anyone, to make a claim against your estate as long as you are living."

Austin winced at the word *consummated* but presumed Allan didn't read his reaction correctly.

"That's not to say she couldn't dig around and find a lawyer to come after a chunk of what you have, but they would have a better chance after you're deceased. At your age, you have a good chance of living as long as or longer than the Rosen woman anyway."

CHAPTER 95

This is all mind-boggling, Austin thought to himself. His mind raced. He was glad he had flown to Columbus to meet with Allan face-to-face. It had been a spur of the moment decision and was only one day after his encounter with Janie—a very passionate encounter, which was extremely confusing to Austin.

Austin Morris had always been and almost always had viewed himself as loyal, reliable, and honorable. He had dated quite a few girls in college but had never intentionally misled them or out-and-out cheated on them. He had never pretended to be dating one girl exclusively and be secretly dating another girl on the side, that is, except for Sasha.

One of the reasons he had wrestled so much with the invitation from Lorena to marry her was that it had seemed a little bit less than appropriate. Although he had admired Lorena more than any person in the world and certainly his love for her was special, it was not the kind of love he felt he should have had for a wife.

With Angela, it was completely different. He truly loved her, loved her at first sight, and never wanted to do anything to hurt her. He had never even looked at another woman, let alone lusted for Sasha or any other woman, from the moment he had met Angela.

Until Janie. It was upsetting to him as he tried to sort out how much of his phenomenal passion for Janie was because she was clearly Lorena's daughter and a younger, more sexually alluring version of Lorena. And what role did the fact that he had never had sex with Lorena, who probably wanted it and certainly deserved it, play in his passion for Janie?

Furthermore, was he in some way reacting to the awkward exchange the other night between Angela and the Werner guy when he had called her Marie?

Maybe his desire was warped or misguided. Maybe he was angry with both Lorena and Angela, his two wives, for not having told him about things that had occurred in their pasts. Lorena's was a huge omission; he suspected Angela's was a lesser one, but he wanted to find out. Maybe after he got through the next few days with the Janie situation, he would simply ask Angela, "What happened in your past that involved Fredrik Werner?"

Or maybe he'd ask Allan to look into Angela's background. Allan could do it or find people who could. One thing about Allan, he was totally trustworthy.

Austin had imagined that a trip to Columbus to visit with Allan would clear up some things about Janie. Also, he had a sort of notion or fantasy that being around Allan for a while, in his presence, might help him conclude that he really shouldn't see Janie Rosen again. That it would only lead to trouble and that he had better shift his sexual thoughts and desires away from Janie and back to Angela, where they belonged.

CHAPTER 96

"You said Len Weiss would have had you do some investigative research had he suspected Lorena might have had a missing heir somewhere," Austin began again. "Maybe I should have you do some investigative research myself. I have reason to believe that Angela, my wife, also has had some questionable things in her past."

"But, Austin, I'm sure that's completely different. Lorena's was a very significant event, a trauma. If you want to find out about Angela's past, you should just ask her. I'm sure she will be fairly open. To engage me in some investigation, some dirt-finding mission would not be a good thing for a man who loves his wife to do."

"You mean if she ever found out, she would lose trust in me?" Austin asked.

"Yeah, partly that, but it would clearly demonstrate to you that you don't trust her—whether she ever found out or not. Besides, healthy marriages are supposed to be built on openness and trust."

"I always thought Lorena and I had a healthy marriage," Austin said, not sure he fully believed what he was saying. "That was, until just recently."

"Your two marriages are completely different," Allan insisted. "The first one had at least a couple of strikes against it from the beginning. Your marriage with Angela doesn't need to have any strikes against it. Don't go behind her back to try to dig up negative stuff about her life before she knew you. Whether it's Angela or Lorena, whatever they did before you came along was history. They're not accountable to you for what they did before they fell in love with you."

Allan always made good sense. He was clearly a wise man, a good advisor.

Austin listened to him, understood what Allan had said, and hoped that his words would diminish or at least temper some of his lustful fantasies about Janie.

He knew he should leave her alone in spite of the overwhelming urges each of them had felt earlier in the week at the Registry's alcove. Damn! He'd never experienced this kind of confusion and sexual dilemma. Maybe he was going through a pre-midlife crisis.

CHAPTER 97

The weekend was somewhat enjoyable, but Austin knew he was distracted. Angela knew it too.

"What's the matter, honey? You don't seem like you're here. What's preoccupying you?"

"I don't know . . . maybe it's this whole business I told you about before I went to Columbus. You know, the Rosen woman shows up out of the blue and is pretty definitely Lorena's daughter. I had no idea. Lorena never told me or anyone about having had a baby as a teenager. She apparently gave the baby up for adoption and totally turned her back on the kid. Even when she was approaching death, she never tried to make any contact with her own flesh and blood. I just don't get it."

"I know, and I don't either," beautiful Angela touched him and tried to be reassuring. "As I look at Samantha, I can never imagine how any parent, mother or father, can just walk away from a child they brought into the world."

With that, she picked up darling Samantha and put her on the combined laps of herself and Austin. She snuggled closer to Austin and murmured, "Family hug!" as she and Austin together wrapped their arms around the baby.

"Did you find out anything that was helpful from Allan?" Angela, too, had great admiration for Allan. She liked him a lot but also knew that he was first and foremost Austin's lawyer and board chairman. If there was ever a dispute between her and Austin, she knew that even Allan could not be an unbiased arbitrator.

"Allan's good, and Allan was very helpful. He assured me that the Rosen lady (he didn't like to use the name Janie in front of Angela) doesn't have any legal rights to part of the estate that Lorena passed on to me."

"That kind of stinks—for her, doesn't it?" Angela asked, reflecting her compassionate nature.

"Yes, I guess. I've been thinking about offering her a financial package, though, enough to take care of her mom who has Alzheimer's. I don't know if she needs money or not."

"You said she seemed sincere when she told you she didn't want money. She just wanted to learn about her mother." Angela remembered.

"Yeah, but Allan said anyone and everyone would not mind having a little more money. So I think I'm going to offer Janie—Ms. Rosen—some kind of long-term financial security. I think I'll call her Monday and drive over to Boca to see her. Do you want to meet her?" He heard himself ask half-heartedly.

"No, not really. But thanks for asking. I think you'll do much better by yourself. Besides, I've got a busy week coming up, and I don't want to get involved in your past life. I just want to be involved in your current and future life," she said and leaned up to give him a loving kiss. Samantha cooed.

"Speaking of the past, did you think any more about that Werner guy who thought he knew you?" Austin saw an opening and took it. "Was he some sort of mystery man from out of your past?"

"Well, actually, he was." Angela knew that she felt nervous and hoped that Austin wouldn't pick up on it. She felt tears building.

"Back in college, I went to a fraternity party down at Ohio U. My girlfriend was supposed to go with me but backed out at the last minute. I met this guy Fredrik, and we ended up drunk and staying up all night together. I used my middle name because I didn't really like him and I didn't want him to try to follow up and find me. Kenny knew where I was, but I felt I was cheating on him with Fredrik. It was wrong, I know, and I was afraid somehow things would get back to Kenny."

"That's okay, sweetheart. I'm sorry." Now it was Austin's turn to reassure as he squeezed and caressed Angela's shoulder.

"I did some things I'm not proud of. In fact, I'm ashamed of them. I told you I always felt guilty about taking money, gifts, and trips from Red Conway, the older gentleman I went with."

Austin knew of Red Conway, the big-time wheeler-dealer in automobiles. The guy who had several franchises in Ohio and Florida. The big, white-maned, booming voiced sales-type who conveyed incredible sincerity through frequent TV spots.

"I'm sorry. I didn't mean to stir up your past, darling. I really didn't." Austin continued to stroke Angela and baby Samantha as Angela cried softly.

"My own past is confusing enough right now. I just want to put all this shit with Lorena's secret-love child behind me. I just want to close this chapter of the book and not read it again, as Allan would say."

Austin was basically glad he had asked Angela about the Werner fellow. She had seemed nervous but, for the most part, had cleared it up. He wondered in his mind how someone as beautiful as Angela could hook up with a chunky, unattractive Germanic lug like Werner. Maybe they had messed around a little, but it didn't sound like they had gone all the way.

Oh well, things happen and cannot always be explained rationally. For example, why did he constantly have to fight his thinking about Janie and fantasizing about making love to her? This had all come on so suddenly. He couldn't keep from visualizing her face, her hair, her dangerously seductive eyes. And he couldn't control his instant erogenous reaction whenever she reappeared in his mind.

"Did you find out anything about the father? You know, Janie Rosen's father?" Angela asked.

Austin had almost a stunned reaction. "No. Allan said the birth record showed L. Wasserman as the birth mother—you know, Wasserman was Lorena's maiden name. But in the box for the father's name, it simply said 'unknown.' I did ask Allan to talk to his father since he's the lawyer who handled the private adoption. He said his father Simon, who's in his 80s now, has a memory that sort of comes and goes. Some days, he remembers details incredibly, and other days, his memory is pretty fuzzy."

"So is Allan going to get back to you?" Angela asked, no longer with tears.

"Yes, he said he'd try talking with Simon this weekend, and if he found out anything, he'd call me this week, probably Thursday. Monday, Tuesday, and Wednesday are Jewish holidays."

"I feel sorry for this Janie woman. I really do," Angela said.

"Why? How so?" Austin asked.

"Whatever life she had before has suddenly been turned upside down. At age forty, or however old she is, she learned that she was adopted. Her real mother, her biological mother, is deceased, and maybe her biological father is too. My father died when I was five, but at least I have a lot of wonderfully warm memories of him, and I feel that he still sort of lives inside of me. This poor woman may never know much about her biological parents. Did she ask you to help her find out who her father was?" Angela asked, obviously with a lot of sympathy or empathy for Janie Rosen.

"Not really. I just thought she'd eventually want to know, and I thought maybe I could help her out," Austin reacted, somewhat awkwardly.

"Please do, sweetie. Please help Janie any way that you can."

CHAPTER 98

It was Thursday, the first day after Rosh Hashanah. Austin was tense in spite of his effortlessly guiding the black luxury Mercedes across Alligator Alley, going from Naples to Boca Raton. He was on his way to meet with Janie, offer her a financial package, and ask her to sign a contract avowing to never come after any additional money—even if he were to die.

He knew it could be uncomfortable to ask her to sign a contract, but he was fairly certain that Janie would be like Angela had been when he had asked her to sign a prenuptial agreement. Angela had herself been very willing and comfortable with the agreement, and that had made it much easier for him.

Austin was trying to think about all kinds of things other than his encounter with Janie as he set the cruise control at eighty-two miles per hour. He wanted to just "play things out" and see what might happen.

He had spoken with Janie by phone on Monday, and she had seemed pleased that he would be coming to see her Thursday. He couldn't read her voice on the phone as well as he could read her overall responsiveness in person.

Two things he knew for certain: one, he wanted to be totally intimate with her, spend the day into the evening naked in a bed. And two, he didn't want to lose what he had—an unbelievable wife and daughter—the "whole package" as his brother Nate once described his older brother's current life.

Why would a man like himself jeopardize what he had when he had pretty much everything he could want? But for some reason, this woman Janie seemed as if she might be worth the risk. She was mysteriously seductive, seemingly without trying to be.

She was intelligent, was a social worker, and understood human suffering, human needs. When he had told her on Monday, "I really need to spend some time getting to know you better. I want to spend all day with you on Thursday," she had responded, "I understand. I feel the same way about you."

When he had told her, "After lunch, I figured we could go to a private room at the Boca Raton Resort to discuss a financial matter—does that seem like too much of a pretense to get you in a bedroom alone?"

She had responded, "a little bit, but I like it."

Janie had gone on to say, "I'm not interested in finances. Maybe I'm like my mother who has always been frugal and who now could never outlive her money, but I'm comfortable, and I did not come to see you to ask for money. Apparently, you have an extraordinary amount, which I do not, but I am comfortable. I'm not sure, but I think Mr. Federer's father, when he set up my adoption—that sounds so strange—was able to set up my adoptive parents, Elinor and Harry Rosen, very well financially. I never knew how Daddy made his money, but I always felt like we were rich or at least well-off."

In recalling their conversation and remembering her calling the only father she had ever known "Daddy," Austin wondered if he had done the right thing by asking Allan to check with his father Simon to see if he remembered who the birth father was. He probably should have thought more about Janie's needs and not have pursued the matter unless Janie eventually asked him to help her.

Digesting a lot of strange information about being adopted, about what kind of mother the person was who gave you up for adoption, was probably difficult. Maybe she should cope with the information she had before digging up additional information.

Suddenly, his mobile phone rang. He saw that it was Allan Federer's private line. Maybe Allan had found out who Janie's biological father was. Maybe it would further "turn her world upside down," to borrow Angela's descriptive phrase.

Austin nervously answered the phone, which brought to a halt his images of Janie and himself, naked and coupled in bed together at the Boca Resort.

CHAPTER 99

Janie Rosen had been feeling totally drawn to this beautiful man, Austin Morris. She felt herself falling in love. Since the trip to Naples, replete with a modern-day Prince Charming and erotic kissing in daytime darkness, she had thought about little else. She had fantasized since their passionate encounter at the Registry that he might finally be the one—the one man, the solid, healthy person with whom she could spend her life.

She found herself writing his name, doodling, and writing her own name with his as she fantasized about the two of them being together alone. She even wrote "Janie Morris" and reacted as an embarrassed, self-conscious schoolgirl.

This is crazy, she thought. Why was she always drawn to men who were not right for her or not available? Years of therapy with Dr. Edberg had helped her entertain a number of hypotheses, including that she didn't feel she deserved a truly good person or that she had enough self-loathing that she set herself up for failure—failure because she chose to pursue goals that she could not attain.

But these sorts of explanations that were offered to explain her occasional forays into the lives of married men were very difficult for her to accept.

She knew that Austin was married, and that was obviously a problem. Years ago, after several months of dating a married man, she had sworn that she would never let herself go down that path again. The path was usually, if not always, fraught with problems of guilt and mistrust.

How could a person be admired and trusted if he or she began a relationship while committed to someone else? The old pickup line, "I'm married, but I don't love my wife," had worked a few times with her, but she had sworn it would not work again. Ever.

But this time, this man seemed different. Austin hadn't talked at all about his wife and whether or not he loved her. In fact, Janie assumed that he probably did. He seemed strong enough and probably rich enough to do whatever he wanted. He hadn't really come on to her; they had *collided* with each other. They had been at the mercy of something beyond themselves, something metaphysical, which had driven the collision.

"This might be some kind of rationalizing," Janie responded in her self-talk. If Dr. Edberg were with her (she wondered if he was still alive), he would challenge this "magical thinking" as being very self-justifying. Damn! He would go on to challenge her to think about why a single woman might be attracted to a married man.

Could it be because the married man is safer, in that there is some degree of probability he will never leave his wife, and therefore, the level of commitment will always be diminished by his unavailability? Or might the "other woman" be seeking to break up a marriage that symbolized the marriage of her mother and father and ultimately steal her "father" away from her "mother"?

Either interpretation did not make Janie feel good about herself. Either way, Janie sensed she was setting herself up for a long-term heartache. She knew, though, from years of experience and numerous relationships that never lasted that her heartache was preceded by primal excitement and sheer passion.

The thrill of endangering oneself at the edge of a cliff had no parallel; that is, no parallel other than the headlong thrust into a relationship that consumed every ounce of thought and energy and returned precipitous pleasure quakings.

She wanted to believe and tried to insist upon believing that this man was different. She didn't want to respond to self-doubts or skepticism. She didn't want to think about what she might be doing to herself. She only wanted to believe. She only wanted to be with Austin as quickly and as long as possible.

Chapter 100

The Temple of Beth Israel in Boca Raton welcomed its attendees with modern architecture on the outside and with conservative, traditional ambience on the inside.

Jews were welcomed with solemn yet subtly celebratory moods as they entered and nodded to one another. Sometimes they shook hands, and sometimes they bowed slightly; occasionally they embraced, but rarely did they linger in their human touching.

Rosh Hashanah was the beginning of the New Year for those of their faith throughout the world. Boca Raton, Florida, was no exception. The temple seemed bursting at the seams to Janie as she entered. She was clad in black as was her mom who clung tightly to Janie as she entered a world that was no longer familiar. Elinor found her own confusion frightening.

The two were nondistinguishable from the throng.

"Why is everyone wearing the same dark colors?" Elinor asked in a rasping voice louder than a whisper.

"This is Hashanah, a day of judgment, Mother. We are beginning a new year, but we are here to reflect on our lives and our sins against God and our fellow man." Janie leaned close to her mother's ear and whispered softly, lovingly. She kissed her softly before she moved away.

Janie had been making every effort to be patient, to be tolerant toward her mother. She tried not to criticize and not to show little signs of exasperation. Her mother had become a child again, hastened by the advent of Alzheimer's. She remembered how she had felt loved and adored by her father—he had never been impatient with her.

Patience was probably the best ongoing gift she could give to her mother at this point—her mother who increasingly did not quite recognize her only daughter. Janie was not about to "shush" her mom or act disapprovingly toward her for asking her question so loudly.

"If it's the start of a new year, shouldn't we all be happy? Too many shades of black, all the same . . ." Elinor's voice was so soft, Janie barely heard her.

The female rabbi stood tall and erect, delivering a message for all who were gathered, but designed to reach as many individuals personally as possible. She spoke of trials, burdens, and false starts. She spoke of centuries of persecution that had befallen all Jews.

Janie heard the rabbi's message and felt as though the message was tailored for her. She knew that Rabbi Minsky had had her own share of disappointments in relationships, so Janie knew they could relate to each other. They had never been together one-on-one, but it now felt as though they were.

"We cannot accept persecution. We were chosen people but not for persecution," Rabbi Minsky softly implored.

"We were selected as the people to interpret God's wisdom, love, and message of hope to all humankind. God knew that we could be trusted to carry the weight of these responsibilities and that our own undying faith would keep us from wavering. But we must be strong. We must be resilient. We must bond with each other through our unifying beliefs."

These words were resonating deeply with Janie as she suddenly admired Rabbi Minsky without reservation. This felt unusual, even rare, for Janie to look up to another woman in such a wholesale way. Janie liked Rabbi Minsky's handsome features, poise, and straightforwardness. She especially liked the deep sense of conviction that she conveyed.

Janie thought it clever and subtle that Rabbi Minsky never referred to God as *he* and that she used the word *humankind* instead of *mankind*. This was a person of exceptional intelligence, almost by definition as a rabbi, and of exceptional strength. And this person just happened to be a female rabbi.

"We have all been disappointed and hurt. And some of us have been the brunt of discrimination. Perhaps even ridicule. Some of us have been used and betrayed. But let me tell you the gravest of persecutions in this twenty-first century. We don't need to return to the death camps of World War II. Many of us continue to be targets or victims. In the view of many French philosophers, 'We are all our own jailers.' What we have done is to constrict ourselves, to confine ourselves. Too frequently, especially we women, have persecuted ourselves. We didn't wait for another person, perhaps an enemy, to put us down. We were *already there.*"

Rabbi Minsky went on to talk about feeling inadequate and feeling less than deserving. Janie absorbed it all, the words and the feelings, and felt as if she were memorizing the message as it was being delivered. At least, its essence would be forever emblazoned within her.

Janie now knew what an epiphany really was. Her whole life was suddenly logical and explainable. Her bad choices and broken relationships were not directly attributable to her mother or to her father or to the two of them together.

They were attributable to herself. She had made decisions and gone with her feelings in spite of yellow flags, red flags, and sometimes thunderous alarms. She had selected men who were not right for her yet had continued to trust her own bad instincts.

Why? And what could she do about it?

She had done so because she had never fully believed in herself or felt as though she deserved a good, mutually satisfying relationship.

She had persecuted herself. She had punished herself. To break the cycle, she had to hang onto the emotion that came with the epiphany. She had to cling spiritually to the awakening of Hashanah. The delicacies she would eat later tonight, as omens of good luck, would need to nurture and sustain her during temptations to fall back into old patterns.

As Rabbi Minsky stepped down and seemed to purposefully make direct eye contact with her, Janie began to cry softly but enough for Elinor to hear and ask, "What's wrong, my darling Janie?"

"I just remembered, Mother—I have to cancel a meeting tomorrow."

"What kind of meeting, sweetie? Is it important?"

"I thought it was important, but now I know it is important not to be there."

"Shalom, my darling Janie. Happy New Year!" Elinor said as she hugged her only daughter.

CHAPTER 101

"You'd better pull off the road to listen to me," Allan Federer instructed Austin the following day.

Austin obeyed, pulling off at mile marker sixty, not too far from the Sawgrass Expressway Exit.

"What's up? You sound ominous again."

Allan seemed to disregard Austin's observation and proceeded humorlessly. "I've spoken with my father several times, and believe it or not, he has dug around in some of his old files at home that he meant to throw away years and years ago but didn't."

"What did he find?" Austin asked nervously. He knew the news was going to be bad.

"I'll just spit it out, Austin, and I'm sorry. Lorena's teenage boyfriend who got her pregnant was a guy who was visiting Cleveland from his hometown of Lancaster, Ohio. He was not Jewish but somehow got involved with her. It was Red Conway—you know, the car dealer. Our firm has done a lot of work for him."

"Oh my god, Allan! This is just terrible, shitty information. Are you sure?"

"Unfortunately, yes. I loaded a couple of crackerjack investigators with lots of money, and they definitely verified it."

"This is just fucked up! I'd like to meet this Conway guy and maybe hammer the shit out of him!"

Allan had known Austin would be upset, but he had never seen him this upset. He'd never really heard Austin use the word *fuck*.

"Let me fly down there, Austin. I want to be there to help. We'll figure this thing out."

"I don't know, Allan. I just need to stop for about two days and do nothing. I have to figure out how I can put all these crazy pieces together. Let's see . . . my beautiful wife Angela, with the blessing of her screwball boyfriend, traveled, had a little bit of sex with, and accepted money and gifts from an over-the-hill bullshit artist named Red Conway. She told me about him, and I told you. She admitted she spent a long evening with this guy Fredrik Werner, but I'm not sure she told me everything. Now out of nowhere, a daughter my first wife Lorena had never mentioned and had literally 'written off' forever shows up and wants to learn about Lorena. Who knows what other secrets are ready to surface?"

"I trust you're still off the road, right?" Allan asked with genuine concern.

"Yes, I am, Allan. I'm all right, and I must say, I appreciate your telling me this. I'm tired of secrets. I'm tired of wives not telling me the truth."

"Well, maybe they have loved you too much. They didn't lie. Technically, they just withheld information. You didn't necessarily ask the right question."

"What do you mean *loved me too much*? They loved themselves and wanted me to think they were wonderful and unblemished."

"Maybe," Allan continued. "But maybe they felt their pasts were not relevant to the present, so why should they burden you? They have known what high standards you have and didn't want you to torment yourself about things that were history. Besides, it's almost impossible to know someone completely. They only let you know what they want you to know," Allan concluded.

"Now you sound like Lorena."

"How so?" Allan asked.

"She always used to say that everyone has some things that only they themselves know. I never agreed with her, but now I think I do."

"Are you going to be all right?" Allan asked.

"Yeah, I guess so."

"What are you going to do now?"

"I'm going to drive into Boca, call Janie Rosen, and meet her for lunch, maybe at Houston's. I just feel like being out in public and finding out if I can help her or her mom in some way financially."

"That's good, that's good. I would suggest setting up a trust for her mother that pays for her round-the-clock nursing care so that she can live at home and not be any kind of hardship for the girl."

"That's a good idea. I'll discuss that with her," Austin responded unemotionally.

"Are you sure you don't want me to come to Boca? I could meet you right after lunch at the airport."

"Maybe that's a good idea. Call me when you land, or I'll call you. I can come right over, directly from Houston's. Maybe I'll bring Janie with me if it seems appropriate."

"Fine. I'll leave here in five minutes."

"And, Austin, I'm really sorry to be the bearer of bad news."

"It's not your fault. Thanks for telling me, and maybe it doesn't have to be so bad. Maybe it's good. Maybe it's going to help me in the long run."

Austin was not even tempted to tell Allan that he had been fantasizing about having sex with Janie Rosen from the moment he had met her, and Christina had conveyed concern through her eyes.

But now he knew he could not and would not make love to her. The whole setup was feeling creepy, even incestuous.

The two most important women in his life had slept with this guy Red Conway. The second one had told him, and the first one hadn't. And now Red Conway's illegitimate daughter was waiting for him in Boca, almost certainly anticipating having sex with him.

How could all this have happened? And how could Red Conway, as a young boy, impregnate Lorena and, years later, as an old man, fuck Angela? Hopefully, the womanizer had never knocked up Angela.

Thank God, at least, he had the news before he climbed in bed with Janie. But now what would he tell her? How would he tell her? Austin wasn't sure yet.

He probably would tell her a version of the truth: that he found her extremely attractive, even seductive, but that he couldn't go through with his desires because he loved his wife. As far as telling her who her real father was, he probably wouldn't.

One thing he knew for certain, though, was that he wasn't going to tell Allan that the call had come just in time—just in time to put the brakes on his cheating on Angela. Allan would never need to know, nor would he, that his father's rooting around in the garage or the attic had saved the sanctity of a marriage.

No, he wouldn't tell Allan how close he had come to being unfaithful. Nor would he tell Angela. These feelings and this day would soon be in the past. The past was not nearly as important as the future. And the best way to take care of the future was to focus on the present.

CHAPTER 102

Janie Rosen was calm and sure of herself as she waited for the phone to ring. Austin had told her he would call around ten thirty in the morning, and she knew that he would be punctual.

She knew that she had to tell him that all dreams of a long afternoon at the Boca Raton Resort were over. She had thought of an elaborate explanation, a truthful one, that involved her telling him about some of her particularly bad choices over the years, the agony she had put herself through, and so on.

In some ways, she wanted him to hear about her discovery at the temple through Rabbi Minsky but then wondered why she would share these kinds of personal, intimate details with someone when she was trying to "cool off" any possible intimacies.

No, it would be better to keep it simple. She could just start with the old line from sitcoms and break-up artists: "It's not you. It's me."

Then she could continue, depending on his reaction with something, such as, "Although I am extremely attracted to you, I can't do this to you and your wife."

Adding that third person, his wife, into the conversation should cool down his fantasies and his libido.

She would do this as soon as he came to pick her up. She wanted to see his facial responses. She didn't want to hurt him, but she wanted to make sure he got the message. She didn't really want to go to a room at the resort but had decided not to totally cancel.

At ten twenty-five, the phone rang.

"Hello?"

"Janie, this is Austin Morris." *Hmm . . . interesting,* she thought. He used his last name.

"Good morning, Austin. I knew you'd be on time."

"You know me too well. Amazing, after such a short amount of time."

"Where are you?" she asked. She could hear in his voice a shift from where he had been emotionally two days earlier.

"I'm getting on the Sawgrass Expressway and should be at your place in forty minutes. There's been a change of plans though."

"Oh?"

"Yeah, I think we should go to lunch at Houston's, the one at Glades and Military Trail, and talk about how I might be able to help you and your mother. You know, financially."

"Well, thanks, but like I've said, I really didn't find you and come to you for money or financial help."

"I know, I know, and I believe you. But as I see it, my first wife, Lorena, was responsible for you and should have done something to help you."

"But she was a young, scared, pregnant teenager who was probably forced to have me. If it were today, she probably would terminate the pregnancy, put it behind her, and pretend it never happened," Janie countered.

"But she wasn't a young teenager forever. She grew up, married well, and ended up extremely wealthy. At some point, I think she should have tried to find you and tried to do something. It seems to me that would have been the responsible thing to do," Austin asserted.

"Maybe so, Austin, but your standards of responsibility are very high. I wouldn't be so hard on Lorena at this point in time."

"You may be right," Austin responded and then went back to the subject of financial help. "At least, let's have the discussion about money. We can have lunch at Houston's for a couple of hours, and then, if we need him, Allan Federer, my attorney whom you know, should be in the area. How does that sound?"

"That sounds good, Austin. It sounds as if you've done a lot of soul-searching."

"Well, yes, some. But I've done most of it this morning on the drive over."

"Good. I'll see you when you get here."

Dr. Edberg, her old therapist, had frequently told Janie that it was good to get feelings out in the open, "on the table" so to speak. In doing so, people were able to be honest and learn to trust one another because they were being authentic.

In her own practice and in her own personal life, for that matter, this had not always panned out. In this situation, she decided she would defer to Austin. His voice, his manner, and the subject of their conversation conveyed one thing clearly: he had decided not to pursue a sexual relationship with her.

There would be no need for her to tell him she had reached the same decision.

CHAPTER 103

Lunch at Houston's was excellent, and the dialogue between them was very straightforward. Each avoided flirtatious looks or suggestive language. They talked business, and she agreed to do whatever Austin and Allan Federer recommended. She asked Austin to have trust papers and any other documents for his protection prepared, and she would sign them.

Janie knew that Allan was on his way to Boca and might even be there already. But she didn't want to see him. She had a feeling, sort of a scary feeling, that Allan had dug into her background and had found out who her biological father was. Allan seemed like the thorough, anally retentive type who would do whatever it took to protect his client, especially Austin.

And clearly, Allan's client was Austin—not her.

But she didn't really want to know. She purposely did not ask Austin if he knew who her biological father was. She loved the only father she had ever known—Harry Rosen.

He had been a good father, a wonderful father. He had always revered her, and to him, she could do no wrong.

She didn't want to find out who the sperm donor was to Lorena Wasserman Weiss Morris. To her, Harry Rosen was her real father.

They ended their lunch on a philosophical note. "Do you think we can ever really know anyone completely?" Austin asked.

"Probably not, but it's probably not necessary. We all have things in our past, even our recent past that are hidden," the intelligent social worker and therapist responded.

"Uncovering all of an individual's personal information," Janie continued, "seems to me to violate a certain kind of ethos or respect for an individual's privacy."

Austin was again struck by her intelligence, her depth. Someone, hopefully, would find her and have a true soul mate as he once believed he had with her mother.

"I wonder if we should even want to. You know, learn everything about someone. In classic whodunits, once we find out the answer, there is no more mystery," Austin said.

"I agree. Life's mystery—its intrigue is really about trying to understand ourselves, who we have become, and what our purpose is. Life's journey is not about trying to uncover all the secrets from the past but rather trying to unlock the opportunities of the future," she responded.

"I understand, and I couldn't agree more," Austin said as they stood up from the table, and he hugged her tightly.

They did not kiss. Austin was suddenly flooded with the same misgivings, the same pangs of guilt and loss he had experienced back when hugging Lorena for the last time.

CHAPTER 104

The drive back west and north across Alligator Alley would be a quick journey for Austin. Luckily, there would be no troopers and no radar traps. After leaving Janie in the parking lot at Houston's, he would feel better.

He called Allan Federer before he got into his car. He watched Janie drive out of the parking lot slowly. She seemed tentative as if she wanted the car to stop and turn around on its own. But it didn't.

"Where are you?" Allan answered his cell phone, with a fatherly tone in his voice.

"I'm here in the parking lot at Houston's. Janie just left, and she is going to sign any and all papers that you send to her."

"I can take them to her right now," Allan—always a man of preparation and action—responded.

"No, don't. Please don't. Just wait a few days after you get back to Columbus and mail them to her."

"Okay, if that's what you want. You know me. I think it's always best to strike while the iron—"

"I know. I know, Allan," Austin interrupted. "But this time, we're dealing with a very special, very sensitive woman—remember, she's Lorena's daughter. I don't want her to read between the lines and think that what we really wanted all along was just to get her to sign off on things so we could forget about her and go on our own merry way."

"That's fine, Austin. I'm sure you have a good feel for her and for what will work best." Austin detected skepticism in Allan's voice but not out-and-out disagreement.

"I just want to bring closure to this and for all of us—me, Angela, and Janie—to move on," Austin said with firmness.

"Hmm . . . I see," Allan said, sensing that there was more to the story than he was getting. "Did you tell Janie we know who her biological father was—I mean is?"

"No, I didn't. I don't really think she wants to know, and I doubt if she ever will."

"Does she know that you know who he is?" Allan kept probing.

"Not really, but I think she senses it. She senses that I know some things about her that she doesn't know, but I don't believe she wants to find out. She's okay with things as they are for now and wants to get on with her life. I think I was helpful to her today."

"That's good. And these financial measures we put in place for her and her mom will only make all that easier."

"That's great, Allan. I appreciate your hard work on all of this. I'm feeling very relieved, very fortunate," Austin said. "And I appreciate your flying down today and sort of being on standby over at the airport."

"You're always welcome, Austin. We just landed a few minutes ago. You want to have dessert at Houston's in five minutes while I come over and get a salad?" Allan asked hopefully.

"No, thanks, Allan. I'd love to, but—no offense—I have a higher priority right now."

"What's that?" Allan asked yet another question.

"I need to go home and see my family, Allan."

"That's *always* a higher priority," Allan affirmed.

"You're absolutely right, Counselor. And I pray to God I never lose sight of that."

And I pray to God I don't start fantasizing about making love to anyone other than Angela, he thought to himself as he headed away from Boca toward Alligator Alley and Naples.

THE END

EPILOGUE

Janie Rosen

Learning of her roots was painful, but it helped Janie think more reflectively about herself and how she had become the person she was. The interactions with Austin reinforced to her that she was capable of relating lovingly and effectively to strong, capable, psychologically healthy men. She looked into the future with hope and optimism, buoyed by Rabbi Minsky's incredibly timely message of self-forgiveness.

Janie began dating Sheldon Ksonska, his divorce well behind him, quite seriously. She knew the relationship offered promise, although she wondered if she could ever feel as complete as she had during her brief relationship with Austin.

Sheldon said that with his connections to investigators, he could help Janie find out who her biological father was, but she said she really wasn't ready.

Elinor Rosen

Elinor became lost in the quagmire of Alzheimer's and, perhaps fortunately, died peacefully soon after Janie agreed to the financial support offer provided through Allan Federer's office.

Fredrik Werner

Fredrik appeared to honor his promise to Angela. He and his wife Joan devoted a great deal of time to their own foundation and to its work providing charitable grants and donations. Fredrik went back to school and earned a PhD in engineering. He and Joan relocated to her hometown in Athens, Ohio, where he was quickly named a full professor at Ohio University.

Allan Federer

Allan Federer continued as the chairman of Lenlor and, from time to time, offered to step aside so that Austin could take over the title. Austin consistently declined, saying he liked things the way they were. Allan's character remained unchanged, and his effectiveness continued without slippage.

Austin Morris

For a short time, Austin was somewhat obsessed with the idea that Lorena had spent her life childless, in spite of having given birth as a teenager to Janie. He appreciated everything Lorena had done for him but, from time to time, wondered why Lorena had never tried to make contact with her daughter Janie. Maybe it would be good, though, not to hold onto such a near-perfect image of Lorena. Maybe it would be better for Angela and for their relationship. He was determined to erase Janie from his memory. Erasing Sasha was more difficult.

Angela Morris

Angela was relieved and felt certain that Fredrik would not reveal their past relationship. She was contacted again by Red Conway, but she asked him to please not reach out to her again as she was happily married.

And she was happily married. She felt it deep within her soul when she was alone, and she felt it every day when she was with her daughter Samantha and Austin. And she especially felt it when she and Austin were alone. No man could ever make her feel as strong, as beautiful, and as loved as Austin did. She loved him because he loved her so much and so unconditionally.

She knew Austin was truly a good man. He was respectful and trusting. He did not ask again about Fredrik Werner.

As far as Angela could tell, Austin's having met Janie Rosen was helpful. She was a social worker and all and maybe had helped Austin accept that his first wife had not been perfect either. In some ways, she was sorry she hadn't met Janie Rosen.

For a few months, Angela considered telling Austin more about the things in her past of which she was ashamed. But then, she thought better of it. She wanted to enjoy her wonderful life with Austin as long as possible—hopefully until death parted them.

Red Conway

Red Conway was busy in Brazil. He quietly sold his dealerships to a private equity firm in Brazil, but the stores never changed the Conway name. He continued as a figurehead and as the spokesperson for the company on radio and television.

He met a beautiful, very young, and very tall Brazilian girl named Giselle. She had completed an MBA program at Harvard. He hired her to be his personal assistant and manager and to travel everywhere with him.

He told Giselle that in a couple of years, when he was further along in his grieving over the loss of his wife, he hoped they would get married. As a token of his love for her and of his future commitment to her, he gave her a 3.5 carat canary diamond ring from Tiffany's. He had taken her to New York to let her pick it out.